J
BRA

Bradshaw, Gillian,
1956-

The land of gold.

$14.00

DATE			

Rec 9/2/93

BAKER & TAYLOR BOOKS

GILLIAN BRADSHAW
The Land of Gold

GREENWILLOW BOOKS, NEW YORK

Map and decorations by Karen L. Baker

Library of Congress Cataloging-in-Publication Data

Bradshaw, Gillian (date)
   The land of gold / by Gillian Bradshaw.
        p.   cm.
   Summary: After the murder of her parents,
a Nubian princess is helped to her rightful
place on the throne by two friendly
Egyptians and the dragon Hathor.
   ISBN 0-688-10576-9
   [1. Nubia—Fiction.   2. Dragons—Fiction.
3. Princesses—Fiction.]   I. Title.
PZ7.B7277Lan   1992
[Fic]—dc20   91-31810   CIP   AC

*Christopher, Michael, and I
would like to dedicate this book,
which we invented together,
to Neville and Jennifer
for them to enjoy when they are older*

Contents

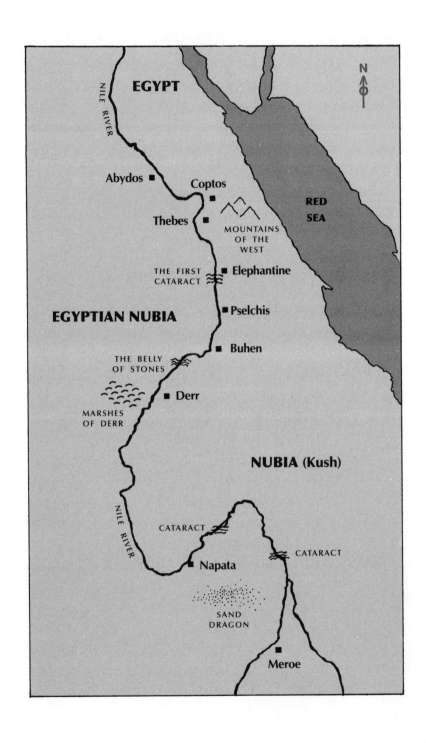

1

Treachery

KANDAKI WOKE IN THE MIDDLE OF THE NIGHT TO THE SOUND OF SCREAMING.

She jumped out of bed and stood still in the dark, listening. Where was the noise coming from? People didn't often scream in the royal palace of Meroë, capital of Nubia. It was a happy place, governed by a kind king and a good queen, and even nightmares were uncommon.

The screams stopped suddenly, but not before Kandaki realized that they were coming from down the corridor, where her father and mother and their servants slept. She pulled a shift over her head and hurried to the door of her bedroom, the blue and gold beads strung on her hair swinging against her shoulders. There was lamplight showing through the doors of her parents' rooms, and she could hear voices talking excitedly. Her father or mother must have had a bad dream. For a king or queen to have a bad dream was a serious thing in ancient Nubia; it might mean that some dreadful catastrophe was going to strike the whole country. They would call the priests to explain the dream for them and to order prayers and sacrifices to whatever god might turn the disaster away. Anxious to know what was going on, Kandaki ran to the doorway of her parents' room.

As soon as she reached the doorway, she knew that disaster was not going to strike; it had struck already. Two of the royal guards lay dead just inside the door of the dressing room. All around them a pool of blood showed dark and shiny in the light of the single lamp in the corner. Another man, a spear sticking out of his chest, was sprawled by the entrance to her mother's room. Kandaki put her hands to her mouth. The world seemed to have turned upside down, and for a moment she couldn't think or move. Then she jumped over the dead guards and ran to her mother's room.

It was full of blood and people, but Kandaki's eyes could take in only one image. Her father and mother lay together on the bed, holding each other, as though each had tried, at the last minute, to shelter the other. And it was clear that both had failed, and both were dead.

Kandaki couldn't breathe. The room seemed to be made of ice, and she thought she would faint. After a long age her stunned lungs took in air in a gasp of horror. The men in the room all looked around quickly. They were all royal guardsmen, she saw, and one of them was Shabako, the captain of the guard. She turned to him with relief. Everyone in the palace agreed that Shabako was the best warrior in the guard, and the bravest. He was a tall, handsome man; when he had become engaged to her cousin Abar, Kandaki had felt a twinge of jealousy. Now she felt certain that he could somehow make things right again. "Shabako!" she cried. "What has happened? Who has done this?"

Shabako came toward her. "Princess Kandaki," he said, smiling pleasantly. "How convenient." Only then did she notice the sword in his hand, its edge dripping blood. She caught her breath as the room turned to ice again.

"It was you!" she gasped, so shocked and stunned that afterward she wondered why she hadn't fainted. "You—you *traitor!*"

Shabako laughed. "Is that any way to talk to your new king, Princess?"

All at once she stopped being frozen with horror and became furious. "You foul, cruel, disgusting, stinking *murderer!* My father *trusted* you!" She leaped at Shabako and tore the sword out of his hand. For a moment he was so surprised that she succeeded in getting it away from him. But he was the best fighter in the royal guard, and she was only a seventeen-year-old princess. He recovered from his surprise and wrenched the sword back before she could stick it in him. Kandaki jumped at him again, tearing at him with her bare hands, scratching as hard as she could. He grabbed her wrists. She bit him. He swore and flung her aside; she caught her head against the wall and slumped, momentarily stunned. One of the other guardsmen, Shabako's second-in-command, Kashta, came and stood over her, raising his spear. She managed to lift her head and stare straight into his eyes. A princess of Nubia, she thought, must die bravely.

"No!" shouted Shabako. "Leave her a moment."

"But she's the only one of the royal family left alive," protested Kashta. "If she stays alive, she'll be a focus of rebellions throughout the country."

"Possibly," said Shabako. "But I want to speak to her first."

Kandaki climbed to her feet, bracing herself against the wall. She saw, with satisfaction, that Shabako's face was bleeding where she'd scratched it, and his hand was bleeding where she'd bitten it. She would let him talk to her. Perhaps she could get him off guard and try for the sword again. Even if his friends killed her afterward, at least she would have avenged her parents. "What do you want to say?" she asked.

He gestured toward the doorway, and she allowed him to show her out of the room. She could hear more shouting and screams now, but they were far away, in another part of the palace. There were four guardsmen with Shabako and Kashta, and she wondered how many others were on his side. Probably most, she realized, with a wave of sickness. As commander of the guard, Shabako would have been able to dismiss all the men who weren't loyal to him.

Shabako showed her into the little room across the corridor that her father had used as an office. Unlike most rooms in the palace, it had a door that could be closed. He jerked his head for Kashta and the others to stay outside and shut the door.

"Princess Kandaki," he said, rubbing the bite on his wrist, "I wouldn't like you to judge me by what you've just seen. It's true I've killed King Arkamon, your father, but I had noble reasons. He was going to hand our nation over to the Egyptians and enslave us all."

"You filthy liar!" Kandaki snapped, too angry to remember that she was supposed to be putting him off his guard. "You know perfectly well he was going to do no such thing. He'd been negotiating a new treaty with Egypt, yes, but that was simply an agreement to help trade, not 'handing us over.'"

"With Egyptians, it comes to the same thing," Shabako said. "They start by trading and end up enslaving. I am a true Nubian and a patriot, and I could not stand by while he betrayed our nation."

It was a lie, a deliberate lie. Kandaki remembered how her mother and father had sat talking together, trying to decide how they could best help Nubian traders in Egypt. She remembered Shabako standing beside them, smiling and pretending to agree. She leaped at him again, but this time he struck her before she could grab the sword. She hit the wall again and this time leaned against it, shaking. It was a wicked lie, but it was one that a lot of people would believe. Nubia had lost wars with Egypt in the past, and many Nubians were afraid to have any dealings with the Egyptians at all. Not only were her parents betrayed and murdered, but people would spit at their names and call them traitors, too. She felt herself starting to cry and made herself stop; she wouldn't give Shabako the pleasure of seeing her in tears. She was wild with shame at the memory of how she used to admire him.

"You're just a dirty traitor," she said. "The only reason you murdered my father was that he was king and you weren't. But you knew that no one would ever support you unless you whipped up trouble with Egypt. Save your lies for your followers, who are too stupid to tell the difference between a real king and a piece of dirt like you!"

"Very well, then!" snarled Shabako, beginning to lose his temper at last. "I wanted to be king. I'm the bravest man in Nubia, the best fighter, and the cleverest general, and it was unjust of the gods to put your father on the throne instead of me. But now I *will* be king. And you can either be dead—or my wife."

"Your wife?" asked Kandaki in disbelief. "You're engaged to Abar. Or have you murdered her, too?"

"Abar is very much alive," Shabako said. "In fact, she expects to be queen. Oh, yes, she knew my plans and has supported me all along. But—" and he lowered his voice—"if *you* would marry me, I'd be perfectly happy to disappoint her."

Kandaki stared at him.

"I've always admired you, Kandaki," he went on, growing smooth again. "You're such a brave, noble girl—not as pretty as Abar, perhaps, but so fine and regal! I always loved you, but I knew your father would never permit—"

"Do you think I'm so stupid I'd believe *that*?" Kandaki exclaimed. "I know why you want to marry me. Kashta just said it. I'm the only member of the royal family left alive, and if you marry me, all the nobles who might have rebelled against you will stay quiet out of loyalty to me. I'd rather die than help you that way. I'd sooner marry a crocodile."

He began to look angry again. "You wild animal!" he snarled. "You always had a vicious temper. Very well, I'll answer you in your own terms. Marry me or I'll kill you."

"Fine!" she snapped back. "I'll go join my parents. The Lake of the Blessed will be our home, and the West, which sinners can't enter. But when it's your turn to die, Shabako, the gods will give you to the Devourer of Shades, and he will gnaw upon your heart in the depths of the underworld forever."

Shabako drew his sword and raised it. Kandaki stepped away from the wall, holding her head high, and waited.

But Shabako lowered the sword again, his eyes narrowing. "You will die," he said, "but I will not kill you." He sheathed the sword and began to smile again. "You seem very concerned about my soul, Princess Kandaki," he said. "It is true that if what the priests say is right, the gods will not be pleased with me for what I've done tonight. I should make them an offering, to soften their anger. And what better offering could I make than a princess of Nubia?"

"The gods don't like human sacrifices," she replied contemptuously. "Send me to them, by all means. I'll ask them to strike you with blisters from head to foot and send worms to eat you alive from the inside out."

"But *some* gods like the taste of blood," Shabako told

her, smiling wider. "There is a god in the north, in the marshes of Derr. They say it takes the form of a dragon. Oh, I see you know of it. Your mother and father, of course, swore that it was not a god at all but a ferocious animal, and they forbade its worship. But if it is a god, it will be grateful to me if I restore its honors and hand it a royal victim. It will protect me from the anger of the other gods. You will do me a favor in spite of yourself, Princess—and I think that will irritate you more than anything else I could do to you."

He flung open the door and went back out to the corridor. "Tie her up," he told Kashta, "put her on a boat, and take her north, to the marshes of Derr. Dress her in all her finery, and leave her as an offering for the dragon of the water."

"Yes, my lord," said Kashta, smiling and bowing. "I will see to it myself."

Kandaki was tied up and hustled out of the palace with a cloak over her head in case someone should recognize her and try to rescue her. The screams and the sound of fighting both had stopped when they reached the royal shipyards, and even through the cloak she could tell that the sun was rising. "The city is ours!" she heard Kashta say to someone at the shipyards, and she bit her lips to stop herself from crying.

Kashta took one of her father's thirty-oared galleys and set out northward down the stream of the Nile in the new morning. Kandaki, still tied up and bundled in the cloak, was dumped in the cabin. When there was nobody to see her, she cried until she was blind and exhausted, and then cried herself to sleep.

It was more than four hundred miles from Meroë to Derr. The galley rowed swiftly downstream through the narrow green valley, slowing occasionally when they reached one of the sections where the river became rough, but always hurrying on again. Kandaki was kept tied up in the cabin and had no chance to escape.

Eight days after leaving the capital, they arrived at Derr, a small white village near the northern boundary of the kingdom. Kashta went ashore and, after a little while, came back with a thin, stooped white-haired man, who beamed and rubbed his hands when Kashta brought him into the cabin and showed him Kandaki.

"This is the priest of the water dragon," Kashta announced. "And this is Kandaki, daughter of Arkamon."

"A princess of the royal house!" exclaimed the old man. "Oh, indeed, indeed, it will like her. Yes, indeed. Why, it has not been given so much as a sick old woman for years and years, and now, a tender young princess! What a change! King Arkamon didn't allow us to give it anything! It has been angry, but now it will be glad. It will eat, and bless you for the offering—you, and King Shabako. I will pray for you, and for the king, my lord."

"I will tell the king of your good wishes," replied Kashta politely. "But now we'd better hurry. The situation in the kingdom is still unsettled, and it would be a calamity if one of the king's enemies learned where we were and stole the victim before the god could take it."

"Indeed!" exclaimed the old man, nodding vigorously. "I will show you the place to make the offering."

The galley cast loose from the bank and rowed upstream a short distance until it came to a place where the Nile had flooded a dip in the land on the west bank, leaving a few square miles of marsh. The tall papyrus reeds nodded in the light breeze, but the water was very black and cold. The galley edged cautiously along the main channel into the marsh. As the oars stirred the water, there was a strange smell, not the normal swampy smell of mud and rotting plants, but a thick, damp, cold smell, a dead smell, like fog in a tomb. The oarsmen shivered, and Kashta was silent. Only the old man smiled.

Eventually they came to a clear space in the reeds where there was a deep black lake. There was no sound except the splash of the oars. No birds fluttered in the reeds, and no frogs croaked from the water. In the middle of the black lake was a heap of stone, and on it stood a stone column about the height of a man.

"This is the place," said the old man, rubbing his hands again.

Kandaki had been watching through a chink in the cabin wall. When Kashta and the old man came to fetch her, she managed to stand up and walk out proudly. But she didn't feel brave. She wanted to cry again.

They had given her some of her own clothes from Meroë, and before she'd been tied she had put them on, wanting at least to die like a princess. As they took her out of the boat down onto the heap of rocks, she glimpsed her reflection in the black water: a tall figure, dressed in white, with gold around her neck and waist, and her hair strung with beads of gold and blue glass. But the face was white-eyed with fear. She straightened her back and set her teeth. I wasn't afraid of Shabako's sword, she told herself. Why should I be afraid of this water dragon? Probably it's just a giant crocodile. It will . . . bite me . . . and that will be that.

The old man brought a metal chain and some thick shackles carved out of wood. He made Kandaki stand with her back against the column, and he fastened one of the shackles around one of her wrists and tightened it firmly with a wooden bolt, which he locked with a heavy black key. Then he led the chain through a hole in the column itself and bolted the other wrist. He stood back and mumbled a long prayer, bowing repeatedly toward the west. Then, raising his head, he whistled—three long, shrill notes that seemed to hang in the still air long after he'd finished. He turned to Kashta. "We must go now," he said.

"Go?" said Kashta. "We must watch and be sure it takes her."

"Oh, no!" said the old man. "No, that isn't wise. You see, it's greedy sometimes." He giggled horribly. "It's bound to be hungry now, after not being given anything for so long. It will want more than one girl. It would smash the boat, and—no, no, we'll go away and come back in the morning. There'll be a few bones then; we'll be sure it's taken her."

"Oh!" exclaimed Kashta, looking about nervously, in case the water dragon decided to come at once. "We'll go now, then." He jumped back onto the boat, helped the old man on, and the oarsmen rowed hurriedly away, pulling with all their strength. Kandaki was alone.

After a moment she began to cry again. It seemed such a horrible way to die, alone in the black marsh. She stood against the column, shivering, and cried until her best dress was damp with tears. "O gods!" she cried, looking at the afternoon sky above her, a pale, clear sky of late winter. "O gods, avenge my parents! Don't let Shabako stay king!"

There was a ripple in the black lake before her. She caught her breath. The ripple drew nearer. Then out of the water just before the heap of stones came the head of a man swimming. He stopped, treading water, glanced carefully about, and then looked at her and smiled.

Kandaki stared back with her mouth open.

"I'm sorry," the man called to her, in the Egyptian language, "I don't speak Nubian. Do you need some help?"

Kandaki shut her mouth with a snap. An Egyptian. She should have realized it at once. His skin was brown, rather than black like hers, and he had the narrow, thin-lipped Egyptian face rather than the wide Nubian one. Why he was swimming in the marshes of Derr, she didn't know, but she suspected that, as a foreigner, he simply didn't know what they were. She spoke Egyptian fluently, and she answered him in that language. "What on earth are you doing here?" she demanded.

"I thought you might want help," he replied. "We saw that galley leave you here, and I thought I'd swim over and see why. If this is part of some ritual to worship the gods, I'm very sorry I've interrupted. But it did look as though you needed help. Are they going to come back?"

"Not until I'm dead," said Kandaki grimly. "And if you stay in that water, you'll be dead as well. You must go at once. What are you doing in these marshes?"

"Hiding," he answered brightly. "But if they've gone, I don't need to." He swam a few strokes closer and climbed out of the water onto the heap of stones. He was a small, thin man, not much older than she, shorter than she, and he was wearing only a linen loin-cloth and a belt. His wet hair stood out in different directions. He turned and waved at the reeds to the north, then turned back to her. "We didn't know how welcome Egyptians were around here, so we thought we'd hide for a while and find out. We only arrived here last night; it was the first good hiding place we'd found since we left the cataracts between here and Egypt. Is it forbidden land or something?" He was examining the wooden shackles as he spoke.

Kandaki closed her eyes, then opened them again. The Egyptian was still there. "You have made a great mistake," she told him. "There is a dragon in these marshes that eats people. The local people call it a god and make offerings to it. I am an offering, and the galley went away because they were afraid to be here when it came. These shackles are locked; you won't be able to save me. You must go *at once* if you want to stay alive."

But instead of being frightened, the Egyptian seemed thrilled. His face lit up. "A dragon?" he asked excitedly. "Here?"

"Yes!" she shouted. "A dragon! And it's nothing to be pleased about! Now go!"

"But I came to Nubia to find a dragon!" exclaimed the Egyptian, grinning with delight. "And there's one at the first place I stop!"

"You madman!" shouted Kandaki. She wanted to burst into tears again. "I have to die, but it doesn't help me for some crazy foreigner to fling himself headlong into death beside me! I don't even know you, but I don't want to watch you die!"

"Oh, dragons won't hurt us," the Egyptian replied confidently. "But why did the people on that galley want you to die?"

She stared at him. Was he really completely insane? He didn't look it; he was working at the wooden shackles like a rational person, trying to loosen the bolts. "Listen," she told him urgently, "you must go away from here. This water dragon has been killing people for hundreds of years. My father forbade sacrifice to it; but my father is dead, and the new king, Shabako, is restoring its worship. What's more, Shabako is going to stir up trouble between Nubia and Egypt. I think you'd better go home as quickly as you can, whatever you came for."

"Your father?" he said. "Who are you?"

"I am Kandaki, daughter of King Arkamon. Shabako murdered him. Look, Egyptian, if you want to help me, go to your pharaoh, and tell him what has happened here; explain to him that, whatever happens, it's Shabako's fault, not all Nubia's."

The Egyptian looked at her seriously. She saw him taking in the gold necklace and the jewels in her hair and remembering the royal war galley that had brought her; she saw him realizing that what she'd said was true. All at once he stepped back a little and knelt, raising his hands as he did so, the way Egyptians did to salute gods and royalty. "In life, prosperity to you, daughter of King Arkamon!" he exclaimed. "I'm sorry. I didn't realize you were a princess." He jumped up again.

Kandaki ground her teeth. "Just get out of here before the dragon eats you!"

"I've told you. Dragons don't eat humans. They think we'd taste revolting."

"How do you know?"

He looked embarrassed. "N-never mind that now. I can't leave you chained like that, Princess. Here, I've brought a saw." And he pulled one from his belt. It was a good copper saw, the kind used to trim date palms. He began to saw through the bolt he'd loosened, on the shackle on her right arm.

She could hardly believe it. "Why did you bring a saw?" she whispered.

"Because I saw you were chained, and I thought I might need to cut you loose," he answered patiently. "We had it on the boat."

"What boat?"

"The one we were hiding, of course!"

She looked out at the black lake. Something was moving in the reeds to the north, the direction to which the Egyptian had waved. A few minutes before, she might have taken it for a monster, but now she noticed the mast of a boat sticking above the reeds, even before the boat's prow pushed through them into the lake. It was an ordinary Egyptian sailing barge, the kind favored by traders, wide in the middle and pointed at either end, with eight oars and a rush-covered cabin in back. Perhaps, she thought, with astonished disbelief, perhaps she might escape. It was too soon for her to feel hope, but the misery in which she'd been sunk gave way to a flood of excited terror.

The man who'd swum out to her kept sawing, and the boat moved slowly across the lake. She saw that there was another Egyptian at the stern, this one a tall man, rowing with one steering oar. There didn't seem to be anyone else on board. Just before it reached the heap of rocks, the first man finished cutting through the bolt, and she slipped her hand out and dragged the chain through the column. She was free.

"I don't know who you are," she said, turning to the Egyptian, "but if you can bring me out of here alive and take me to one of my father's friends, I will load your boat with treasure."

"Well, actually . . ." began the Egyptian, but Kandaki was already scrambling toward the boat. The Egyptian followed her reluctantly.

"Quickly!" she shouted to the man in the back, jumping in. "There's a dragon in the water here, and we must get away before it comes!"

Then she screamed, for a long, narrow gold-eyed head, a dragon's head, had just poked out of the cabin.

2

The Water Dragon

KANDAKI BACKED AWAY. THE SET OF SHACKLES WAS STILL BOLTED TO HER LEFT arm, and she swung it hesitantly, wondering if she could use it as a weapon. The green head came toward her, followed by a long green neck, a pair of powerful claws, and a body masked by a pair of half-folded wings. Kandaki glanced around, looking for a way to escape. She saw only the two Egyptians. The man in the stern just looked bewildered, but the one to whom she'd spoken seemed embarrassed.

"This was a trick!" she shouted, suddenly more angry with him than afraid of the dragon. "You couldn't just leave me to die; you had to let me think I was getting away first! Isn't there any limit to Shabako's cruelty? How much did he pay you for this?" Turning her back on the dragon, she jumped off the boat and, swinging the shackle, leaped at the Egyptian.

He ducked backward into the water. Swinging the wooden cuff at his head, Kandaki ran after him. The other Egyptian gave a shout and waved the oar, and the dragon hissed loudly; but Kandaki paid no attention. The Egyptian dived under the water and disappeared. Kandaki stood still, swinging the shackle and looking about wildly. The Egyptian came up on the other side of the boat.

"It isn't a trick, Princess!" he shouted, treading water and looking at her earnestly.

"Of course, it isn't," said a strange voice—a soft, hissing, rushing voice. "And if you hit Prahotep, I will fly you over to where the mud is deepest and drop you."

With a shock Kandaki realized that it was the dragon that had spoken. She stared at it in amazement, and it stared back unblinkingly with its golden eyes.

"You said there was a dragon here?" it asked her.

"But ... you ..." she whispered, "you *are* the dragon here, aren't you?"

"Hathor is *another* dragon," explained the first Egyptian, Prahotep. "That's why we came to Nubia. She was the only dragon left in Egypt."

"Is there a dragon here?" repeated the dragon. "In this foul-smelling place? It's not the sort of place I'd choose to live, but I suppose he has to hide here or the local humans will kill him."

"No," said Kandaki. "It kills them—eats them. It's the water dragon of Derr. The local people call it a god and offer it human sacrifices."

The dragon curled its lips—her lips, Kandaki supposed; Prahotep had called it she. "Dragons don't eat humans," she declared firmly. "And they don't live in water. Sssss! The thought makes my wings ache. If this creature really eats humans and lives in water, it's not a dragon at all. But if it is a dragon, the humans must have killed their human sacrifices themselves and blamed the dragon for it. That's a typically human thing to do." Then she hesitated and half opened her wings. "Though there is a strange smell here," she said reluctantly. "I said so when we arrived. Not a marsh smell or a human smell, far less a dragon smell. It smells dangerous."

"It's the smell of death," said Kandaki. "Please, let's get out of here. As I said, if you can bring me to safety, I'll fill this boat with—oh!"

She had knocked against one of the big earthenware jars that filled the boat, and it tipped over, spilling out a pile of gold and precious stones.

"That's Hathor's treasure," said Prahotep, as he climbed back into the boat. "You see, the boat's full already. But you can give us something else if you like." He turned to the tall Egyptian. "Baki, she said that the reason the galley left so quickly was that they were afraid of this water thing, whatever it is. I think maybe we'd better take the *Lady* back toward the river, so we can get away quickly if the whatever it is turns out to be unfriendly."

He went to the other stern oar and pushed the barge away from the heap of rocks.

"The lady!" exclaimed Kandaki. "I'm a princess, not a lady! And you must get away quickly before the whatever it is turns up at all!"

"He meant the boat," said Baki. "She's called the *Lucky Lady*. Are you really a princess?"

"Yes!" she shouted frantically. "And please, can we get away?"

"We have to see first whether this thing is a dragon or not," said Prahotep, beginning to row. The boat turned toward the channel and began gliding slowly across the black lake. "We've come all the way from Egypt to find a dragon; we can't just run when one turns up. What does this water whatever look like?"

"I don't know! I've never seen it! I've never heard that anyone's seen it and lived. Please, let's go!"

Baki sat down and also began rowing. The boat moved a bit faster. They had almost reached the channel now.

Suddenly Hathor gave a long, loud hiss. Prahotep and Baki stopped rowing and stood up to stare. Something was moving at the far side of the lake.

A white fog appeared in the reeds. Even from the other side of the lake they could feel the chill. Then the black water rippled in a thick, oily way. The ripples moved toward the heap of stones.

"I don't like this," said Baki. "I think the lady—I mean, princess—is right. Let's get out of here." He sat down and began rowing again. But Prahotep remained standing, watching, merely holding the boat straight with his own oar.

With Baki rowing, the *Lucky Lady* glided into the channel. At the same moment the ripples reached the heap of stones. They stopped. Everything was still for a moment.

Then a huge, pale shape thrust itself up out of the

water. It had a swollen, misshapen head, the color of decay, with great bulging ridges over the eyes and under the enormous, gaping mouth; a slimy fin trailed from the deep folds of its back. A pair of pale tentacles felt at the column where Kandaki had been chained a few minutes before. They seemed to pat the stone for an age, and the monstrous head turned this way and that, as though it knew that someone should have been there. Then there was a noise like mud falling in mud. The white fog swirled, the tentacles clenched at the column of stone, and with a crack the stone broke.

"That is not any kind of dragon," said Hathor. "It's a—sssss—there isn't a word in Egyptian. A cold thing, an underworld thing. It's very stupid and very dangerous. Row *hard.*"

Prahotep bent to his oar, and so did Baki. The *Lucky Lady* began to move swiftly away from the black lake and its hideous inhabitant.

But the splashing of the oars seemed to have alerted the monster to their presence. The horrible head turned toward them—and vanished. Then the ripples began to move in their direction. They moved horrendously fast.

Prahotep was looking quickly around. Suddenly he twisted the steering oar so the boat slewed hard to the left, out of the deep black channel and into the reeds.

"What are you doing?" cried Kandaki. "You'll run us aground!"

"I'll run it aground, too," he answered, still rowing hard. "You saw it. It's a kind of big fish. It can swim faster than we can, but it can't leave the water."

The dragon had climbed onto the top of the cabin, fanning her wings and hissing. The *Lucky Lady* sped over the reeds, dragged a moment, sped on. The ripples in the water paused where they had turned out of the channel, and the fog grew thicker. Then it began to follow them again. When it reached the place where the boat had dragged, there was a sudden spasm, and the monstrous body heaved up into view, flopped heavily through the mud, and descended again. Prahotep twisted the steering oar once more, and the *Lucky Lady* dragged heavily across another muddy patch, slowed, stopped. The mist sped toward them. But when it reached the shallows, it hesitated.

Then the monster heaved into view and began thrashing itself across the shallows toward them, moving like a fish in a puddle. One of the pale tentacles coiled about the boat's prow. Baki gave a yell, drew a sword, and charged toward it. He hacked at the tentacle furiously. There was another horrible noise, and the tentacle twisted like a worm, oozing an icy fog. Baki yelled again and swung his sword harder; the tentacle broke in half. The end fell into the reeds, writhing.

The dragon gave a piercing hiss and leaped into the air, wings thundering. She dropped down on the monster, her claws extended. Deep into the hideous head the talons sank, and her green head snapped at the horrible white, fishy eyes. The monster made a noise of surprise and pain. It thrashed madly, trying to turn back toward the deep water, fog billowing from its mouth. It rolled; the dragon leaped up and swept down again, tearing at its belly. But the remaining tentacle coiled about her, pinning down one wing, and the creature flopped, holding her, toward the lake.

"No!" shouted Prahotep. "No, it mustn't get to deep water!" He jumped out of the boat and splashed through the mud toward the monster. "Hathor!" he shouted. "Hathor, *make a fire!*"

The dragon's head came up. She stopped tearing at the monster and sat still for a moment, curving her neck and staring at the reeds between her and the lake. The water thing gave a triumphant bellow and flopped once more.

Then the reeds burst into flame. The bellow became a whistle of anguish. The horror flopped madly back into the shallows. It let go of the dragon, and she struggled up into the air again. She landed on the roof of the cabin, trembling; again she curved her neck and stared at the reeds, this time at those in which the monster was actually lying. Again there was a burst of flames. Fog poured out, rising in a column of white steam. The thing flopped and thrashed; there was a horrible stink of burning. Prahotep splashed back toward the boat.

"We'd better push the boat clear in case it rolls on top of us," he said. "Princess, we need your help."

Kandaki jumped down into the mud, with Baki, and the three of them shoved the grounded barge with all their strength, their feet slipping in the mud. Behind them, the steam and the stink grew, and the whistling became steadily louder and shriller, until it was almost unbearable. The *Lucky Lady* gave, stuck, gave again. She slid over the shallows. Her prow was turned toward the channel, and she came free. Prahotep leaped in and grabbed the steering oar. He was already rowing when Kandaki and Baki tumbled onto the deck. Behind them the fog boiled, and the monster rolled over and over, back and forth across the place they had just left, but the *Lucky Lady* was gliding smoothly now, back onto the deep black water. As Prahotep turned her prow toward the river, the whistling reached a pitch so high the whole air seemed to shriek, and then there was a kind of pop! and it stopped.

They looked back. The white fog was gone. There was only a smoldering in the reeds—and a huge bulk lying motionless, torn as though something inside it had burst. Greenish smoke oozed from its side.

"I should think that's poisonous," said the dragon. "I'm glad we're upwind of it." She climbed down from the roof of the cabin and rubbed her wing with her head. She was still trembling.

Prahotep let go of the steering oar and went over to her. He stroked the wing. "Are you hurt?" he asked anxiously.

"No," she answered. "Just bruised. But I *hate* water, and the—sssss—nearly drowned me."

"It's a good thing you thought of grounding us, Bad-luck," said Baki. "If that thing had come at us in deep water, we wouldn't have had a chance. But what did you think you were doing, running at it like that? You didn't even have a knife, let alone a sword!"

Prahotep gave a rather shaky smile. "I don't know. I suppose I meant to hit it with the saw."

"It was very brave," said Kandaki.

Baki looked at her irritably. "Of course, it was brave—but it was stupid! Bad-luck's cleverness could knock the feathers off a falcon, but he can be remarkably stupid when it comes to fighting."

"If it hadn't been for Hathor," said Prahotep solemnly, "we'd all be dead."

"And I shouldn't have needed *you* to tell me to make fire," said the dragon a bit acidly. She seemed to be recovering. "But I haven't done it much for a long time. And I've never fought one of those—sssss—before. There weren't many of them around even when I was a fledgling, and I didn't think there were any of them left. Not that I would have gone looking for one. It tasted foul." She licked her lips with a long red tongue. "They're underworld creatures. They have ice for blood. My claws are frozen." She began licking them.

Kandaki sat down heavily. She was covered with stinking mud, and she was so amazed and bewildered she hardly knew who she was. She stared numbly at the water dragon of Derr. "People near here thought that thing was a god," she said.

The dragon hissed. "Humans have a very perverse idea of what a god is."

"I suppose that if they thought it was a god, we can't go to the nearest village, tell them we've killed it, and be rewarded with a feast," said Baki wistfully. "That's a pity."

The dragon nodded. "It's two days now since we ate the oxen," she said sadly. "Princess-human—whoever you are—do you know if it's safe for us to buy food here? We have some nice linen clothing Prahotep thought we could trade."

Kandaki started to laugh. She laughed until she realized that she was becoming hysterical and covered her mouth with her hands to make herself stop. "My parents were murdered eight days ago," she said. "I was left here for that—that *thing* to eat. I've just seen it killed, I don't even understand *how* it was killed, and I'm sitting in a sailing barge with two crazy Egyptians and a dragon. I can't worry about linen clothing." Then she took her hands away from her face and said, "But no—no, of course, it isn't safe for you to buy food here. I do know that. I was telling your friend—Prahotep?—that Shabako, who has usurped my father's throne, is trying to stir up trouble with Egypt so that he can unite Nubia behind him. He'd be delighted if a couple of Egyptians appeared suspiciously out of nowhere. You could be arrested, and he could claim you confessed to all kinds of Egyptian plots against Nubia before he had you executed as spies."

Prahotep winced, and Baki swore. The dragon licked her lips unhappily.

"What's more," Kandaki went on slowly, "the galley that left me here will be back in the morning. Kashta—that's the man in charge of it—wanted to be certain I was dead. When he finds that"—she gazed at the immense bulk in the reeds—"when he discovers that the monster died instead, he'll have every boat he can find looking for me. And if they do find us, we'll all die."

Her heart began to beat faster as she thought of it. The two Egyptians looked at her unhappily, and suddenly she felt guilty. They'd saved her life, but in return all she was doing was putting their lives in danger. "Perhaps you made a mistake freeing me," she told them, steeling herself. "You should return to Egypt and leave me to—to find some of my father's friends on foot."

"We can't go back to Egypt," said Baki. "We're wanted by the temple police. And even if we weren't, we don't have anything to eat on the way. And even if we did, we haven't found another dragon."

"Why do you want to find one so much?"

"If your parents and all your people had been murdered," said Hathor sharply, "and you had been living on your own for five hundred years, and you suddenly heard that there were others of your kind in Nubia, wouldn't you go to look for them? *Are* there dragons here, other dragons like me? Or are they all monsters like that water thing?"

"I don't know," said Kandaki, blinking. "Where did you hear that there were dragons here?"

"I told her I'd heard that there were dragons in Nubia," said Prahotep apologetically. "All the stories call Nubia the land of gold and of dragons."

"But what does it have to do with you?"

Prahotep looked worried. "Hathor's my friend," he said, as though this were obvious. "She saved my life. Of course, I want to help her. Do you mean, there *aren't* any dragons here after all?"

"Well, there are *stories* about dragons in Nubia.

There's the one about the earth dragon of the mountains that killed the Great Wizard. And there are tales of the sand dragons in the eastern desert, and the fire dragons in the south, but whether they're dragons like Hathor or whether they're creatures like the water dragon, I don't know. But even if you succeed in getting away from here alive, you won't be able to wander about Nubia checking on them just at the minute. There's going to be a war."

"With Egypt?" asked Baki. "This Shabako's a fool if he wants to fight Egypt. We Egyptians have beaten you Nubians every war we've fought."

"Not easily!" snapped Kandaki. "You've paid heavily for every victory. And if our numbers were as great as yours, we'd have won every time. But if I have anything to do with it," she continued grimly, "it will be a war against Shabako. If my father's friends know I'm alive and free, they'll join me in trying to overthrow that murderous usurper and restore the royal house."

Baki looked at her in surprise. "*You* want to start a war against a man who expects to fight *Egypt*?" he asked. "With all respect, Princess, aren't you . . . well . . . what I mean is, soldiers prefer a seasoned general to a girl when it comes to someone to lead them into battle. Wouldn't you be better off going north and asking Pharaoh to help you? Even if he didn't lend you an army, he'd probably let you marry one of his younger sons, and you could live very royally in exile."

"Do you think I'd betray my people?" Kandaki demanded angrily. "I would never summon an Egyptian army into Nubia, never! And I'd never sit in Thebes getting fat while my father's murderer tyrannized my father's subjects! No, I'll see Shabako overthrown or die trying. And my house has ruled Nubia for two hundred years; people will support me. Of course I know soldiers prefer to be led by an experienced general, but some of my father's friends *are* experienced generals."

"Where do your father's friends live?" asked Prahotep.

She thought quickly. Every noble in the country, as well as the mayor of every village, had sworn loyalty to her father. But that didn't count; Shabako had sworn loyalty, too. And now he had stolen her father's throne, told lies about her father, and wanted her dead. As soon as he knew she'd escaped the water dragon, Shabako would undoubtedly offer a reward to anyone who killed her and decree fearful punishments for anyone caught helping her. How many people would be loyal now? Some, surely. *Some* Nubians would remember how kind and just her father had always been and would refuse to believe the lies, but which ones? Here, near Derr, maybe most; people here must be grateful to her father for banning sacrifices to the water dragon.

But even here there would be spies. It would not be safe for her to go to the nearest village, announce herself, and expect help. She would have to travel in secrecy. Yes, but travel where?

Of those who might still be loyal, one name stood out from the rest: Lord Mandulis, governor of Napata. Uncle Mandu she'd always called him, though really he was only a friend of her father, not an uncle. She remembered him, a tall old man with woolly white hair, sitting beside her in the garden when he'd come to Meroë and trying to show her how to carve wood. He'd made her a little wooden horse and chariot when she was six. It had been her favorite toy for years. His eyes had always been so warm, and his hands so gentle, that it had come as a surprise to her to discover that he was one of the most famous warriors in Nubia. "I'll go to Napata," she said aloud. "I can trust Uncle Mandu."

"I've heard of that city!" said Baki, surprised. "My grandfather helped sack it the last time there was a Nubian war. It's a few hundred miles upstream, isn't it?"

Kandaki looked at him sourly. She'd heard plenty of stories about the time the Egyptians had invaded and sacked Napata. "Yes," she said.

"What would be the best way to get there?" asked Prahotep. "If you think you'd be safer on foot, Princess, then we'll leave you to make your own way. But if you want to sail, you can come with us—if Hathor agrees, that is. It's her boat."

She looked at him. "*I* can come with *you*? Didn't I tell you that you'd do better to leave here altogether?"

He smiled and shrugged. "Well, we have to go look for these other dragons, you see. It's like Baki said, we can't go back. So we have to sail on upriver, and we might as well go to Napata. It sounds as though we are going to be in the middle of this war, and if that's the case, we've got to choose sides. But we're on your side already, and it's too late to do the choosing. We could help you, you know. I've thought of a way to put that Kashta off your trail. And you'd be a great help to us."

For a moment Kandaki said nothing. She knew nothing about these people. The two men were Egyptians, traditional enemies of Nubia, and they'd just admitted that they were wanted for some crime in their own country. As for the dragon—what was she to think of her? Would her father have approved of a dragon's wanting to move into Nubia and settle down with some other dragons? He would have killed it as a dangerous menace.

Kandaki sighed. It was no use; as Prahotep said, they were already on the same side, and it was too late to do the choosing. She already liked all three of them. "I would love to travel with you," she said honestly. "It's a long way to Napata, and . . . I've never been on my own. I've always had my parents, servants, guards—all of that. I'm not frightened," she added quickly, and not quite so honestly. "But I'd be very glad to sail with you. If we reach Napata safety, I will load your boat with tr—that is, I'll see that you're richly rewarded for your help. And if we defeat Shabako, I'll give you men to help you search for dragons."

"That's a bargain!" exclaimed Baki, grinning. "At least, it is as far as I'm concerned. What do you say, Hathor?"

The dragon's tongue flickered. She rubbed her head against her foreleg. "Prahotep?" she asked, looking at the little man.

"It was my suggestion," he told her. "Since we can't

look for dragons freely, I think it's the best thing to do. But perhaps it would be better if you left us with the *Lady,* and flew to look for dragons on your own. We could arrange a time and place to meet—"

"If we're all still alive," she finished sourly. "No. I'm not leaving you—or my treasure. Very well, we will help the princess as far as Napata. But I'm not getting involved in any human wars. Your kind can kill each other perfectly well without any help from me."

"That's settled then," said Baki with satisfaction. Grinning, he offered Kandaki his hand, and she shook it. "And you watch," he added. "We'll reach Napata. Bad-luck will think of something."

"Why do you call him Bad-luck?" asked Kandaki.

"I wish he wouldn't," said Prahotep.

Baki grinned even wider. "That's what they called him when we first met. It used to be he had bad luck of his own. But now he's bad luck for his enemies. You'll see."

3

Lies and Disguises

 "NOW," SAID KANDAKI, "WE OUGHT TO GET AWAY FROM HERE QUICKLY, BEFORE KASHta comes back."

But Prahotep shook his head. "If, as you say, Egyptians aren't welcome here and Kashta would arrest us on sight, we have to hide somewhere. He has a thirty-oared galley and can get pilots who know the river. He'll travel much faster than we can, and even if we started now, we could never stay ahead of him. And this bit of marsh is the best hiding place for miles. It's big enough to conceal a boat twice as big as the *Lucky Lady,* and no one wants to search it. And I told you, I've thought of a way to put this Kashta off your trail. You said he was coming back to make sure you were dead. What does he expect to find?"

"He *doesn't* expect to find the body of a water monster, that's certain!" snapped Kandaki. "And whatever else you do to mislead him, he'll be pretty suspicious when he sees it."

"But what if he doesn't see it?" replied Prahotep.

"Now, I know, he couldn't miss it. It's in the shallows and near the entrance channel. But we could shift it; it's half in water, and the mud's slippery. We can take the *Lady* near enough to tow, and if that fails, we all can push. If it sinks in deep water, good; if it doesn't sink, we can hide it in the reeds on the other side of the lake. You said this Kashta was afraid to meet it. If he thinks you're dead, he won't stay and look for it—or us."

"Why would he think I was dead?"

"Well, that's what I asked you. What does he expect to find?"

"The old man—the priest—said something about bones. . . ." Kandaki trailed off, staring. "You mean, leave some bones on the heap of rock in the middle of the lake?"

Prahotep grinned. "Exactly! And I thought you could tear that dress up, and we could batter the necklace a bit, and maybe you could cut off just a little of your hair and leave them all on the rocks. Then we take that other shackle off you, thread it through the hole in the stone column, and when Kashta comes back, he sees the remains of the princess, just as he expected. He goes home and tells his master that all is done, and we slip quietly up the river behind him without anyone looking for us."

Baki beamed proudly. "Told you he'd think of something," he said to Kandaki. "But what are we going to do for bones, Bad-luck?"

"Animal bones," replied Prahotep. "If we split them and break the ends a bit, it should pass. They'd expect most of the bones to be at the bottom of the lake anyway. And that will solve our other problem, too; we'll eat the animal the bones come in. We can buy a couple of goats, I think."

"But we can't go into the villages to buy things here," Baki protested. "The princess just said—"

"*We* can't go into the villages, but *she* can!" Prahotep said triumphantly. "She's Nubian, and if she takes off the jewels and the necklace, no one will pay any attention to her. That's right, isn't it, Princess?"

Kandaki choked. She put her hand to the blue and gold beads strung in her hair. Prahotep had already casually suggested that she cut some of it off, tear up her best dress, and smash her necklace. "Do you expect me to crawl about looking like a peasant woman?" she demanded angrily.

He looked surprised. "Of course. You can't expect to go secretly as far as Napata dressed like that!"

She bit her lip. She had faced Shabako like a princess; she had tried to face death like a princess. Now they wanted her to go into a village and buy goats like a peasant woman. Somehow that seemed harder to face than the other two. What if she were caught while she was in disguise? How could she die nobly with everyone laughing at her?

"We have lots of spare clothes," Prahotep went on. "Women's things, too. We bought a whole load of clothing in Buhen, just before we left Egyptian territory. I was planning to trade them here; now you can choose something to wear yourself and trade some of the rest—"

"I'm a princess of Nubia, not a dirty trader!" shouted

Kandaki. "I don't know anything about *buying* things! A member of the royal house doesn't haggle over goats. And I don't want to wear your filthy linens from Buhen!"

Prahotep's face fell. He sat down beside the dragon. "Of course," he said after a silence. "I was forgetting that. I wouldn't expect a pharaoh's daughter to buy goats, and I shouldn't have expected it of you. I'm not used to royalty. Well, I suppose I could dive and see if there are some bones on the bottom of the lake. And I could try to catch some fish to eat tonight."

"You won't catch anything here," said Hathor. "The water thing will have swallowed everything living anywhere near the marsh."

Prahotep sighed. "Well, then, we can eat sedge roots, and you'll have to go hunting."

Hathor looked at Kandaki and hissed angrily. "I don't dare hunt near the river, and the hunting's bad in the desert. I'd be lucky to catch a scrawny old fox."

"Don't you have anything to eat on this boat?" asked Kandaki.

"No," said Baki gloomily. "We started from Thebes with a lot of grain and oil. But we bought some oxen in Buhen, and we had to feed them on the way over the cataracts they call the Belly of Stones; that used up all the grain. When we got to the end of the rapids, we found the boat had sprung a leak, and we had to stop to mend it. That used up the oxen; there were only four of them, and Hathor eats half an ox at one go. So all we've got is sedge roots from the marsh and oil—unless

Hathor can catch something. But don't worry, Princess. Bad-luck only thought of asking you to help because you were so quick to push the boat. Really, we don't expect royalty to do anything useful."

"What do you mean?" she demanded indignantly. "Are you saying I'm useless?"

"I mean, nobody expects you to do anything like hunting or fishing or making linen or buying or selling or baking or brewing or fighting," said Baki soothingly. "Any common trade. I'm sure you're very good at . . . whatever royals do."

Kandaki looked at the dead water monster and pulled the beads on her hair. She realized that what royals did—rule, judge, and lead in war—was pretty useless when it came to producing anything to eat. It annoyed her—and she realized that she was very hungry. Moreover, Prahotep was quite right; she couldn't expect to go secretly all the way to Napata dressed as she was. "Oh, very *well*," she said at last. "I'll wear your dirty Egyptian linen and go buy your stinking goats."

They all smiled again. "I'll fly you to a place near the village downstream," offered the dragon. "It's getting late, and you don't want to buy things in the dark."

"But first," said Prahotep, "we need to disguise you."

The first thing was to saw through the bolt on the remaining shackle, which Kandaki still had on her left arm. When that was done, Kandaki reluctantly cut off three locks of her beaded hair, using a jeweled knife from the treasure in the boat. Then she began untying the knots on the ends of the other locks and pulling off the beads. She was so accustomed to their weight and the way they swung about her head when she moved that when they were off, she felt as though she'd gone bald. She tried not to think about it and went to look at the linen clothing on the boat.

There was quite a lot of it: kilts and cloaks and long white shifts. There was also, to her amazement, a lion skin. She picked it up and saw that it had a gold pin in it so that it could be used as a cloak. "How on earth did you get this?" she asked. "Lions are sacred to the god Apedemek, the patron of my house. We have a law that says no one but a king may hunt them!"

"What a stupid law!" said Hathor, yawning. "I hunt them all the time. A fat old lion that had a lot of lionesses to care for him makes very good eating. The lionesses tend to be a bit tough. I gave that to Prahotep; you put it down."

"I don't suppose I can wear it here if lions are sacred to the king," Prahotep said sadly. "It would probably be safer to get rid of it."

Kandaki, still feeling rather shocked, turned back to the linens. She chose a plain white shift and went behind the boat to wash the mud off herself and change. When she'd put on the shift, she looked at her reflection in the black marsh water. Her hair, still crinkled from the beads, stood out in an untidy mass around her head, and her wide, bony black face looked very plain and ordinary, not like a princess of Nubia at all. Suddenly she wanted to cry again. Angrily she splashed some water over her head to straighten her hair and went back to the others, clutching her old dress and necklace in a messy bundle. She threw the bundle into the boat and grabbed a handful of the linens. "There!" she said. "I'll go buy your miserable goats."

"Right," said Prahotep. "You ought to be able to get one goat for a kilt, or two for a dress or cloak. And it would be good if you could buy some bread as well."

"And some beer," added Baki.

"You can tell them that you're with a party of traders that's camped by the palm grove," Prahotep went on. "We've found it's good to say something vague like that because everyone thinks he knows where you mean. Will you be all right?"

"Yes," she said tightly.

"Good," said Hathor. "Climb on my back, and we'll go."

Reluctantly Kandaki climbed onto the dragon's back, putting the linens underneath her. She wrapped her arms about the green neck. The scales weren't cold and slimy, as she'd half expected, but warm and smooth. She could feel the muscles rippling underneath them. Hathor tensed herself, then jumped out of the boat. Like a swan taking off, she ran along the marsh in a series of bounds, her wings booming and her tail thrashing. Kandaki gasped at each jolt. She closed her eyes, set her teeth, and held on tightly.

The bounding stopped. After a moment the frantic wingbeats evened into steady flapping. Kandaki opened her eyes. They were flying over the marsh, going inland.

Glancing behind, she could see the dead water monster and Prahotep and Baki, small as dolls, aboard the *Lucky Lady*. The lake vanished behind them, and a green stretch of reeds. They rose higher, over the edge of the marsh and on toward the red soil of the desert beyond, climbing higher with each beat of the wings.

"Why are we going this way?" gasped Kandaki breathlessly. "There are no villages here."

"We need to catch the wind," replied Hathor. "You always get a good updraft over the desert in the afternoon—ahhhh! Here it is."

The wings stopped beating and stayed still. The bones in them, cunning as fingers, stretched the golden web of skin outward. Hathor began to turn in a series of lazy circles, up and up into the orange evening light. Kandaki saw the desert unfold westward, and eastward, across the marshes, the river lay enfolded in green. "I like to go up out of sight before I fly over a village," explained Hathor. "The last thing we want is a lot of human attention . . . I think we're high enough now." Easily she turned back over the marshes, gliding with motionless wings. The *Lucky Lady* was tiny now; it had moved beside the toylike monster and was trying to drag it out of the shallows. Baki and Prahotep were almost too small to see. Downstream Kandaki could make out the village of Derr, surrounded by fields and date groves, with men walking behind oxen no bigger than ants, and Kashta's thirty-oared galley, like a miniature toy, drawn up beside the village. Hathor drifted toward it.

"We can't stop there!" Kandaki told her anxiously. "Kashta will be there. Go upstream."

The wings beat once, steadied, and they turned and were going upstream. Kandaki's eyes watered, stung by the wind. It was more wonderful than she'd thought anything could be.

Another village, smaller than Derr, appeared far below, on the eastern bank of the river. Hathor circled above it. "There's a date grove there with nobody in it," she said. "That's a good landing place. Hang on!"

She folded her wings, and they fell steeply. Kandaki cried out, clinging to the dragon's neck with all her strength. The date palms sped toward them, feathery fronds tossing. A few feet above them, the gold wings opened, and there was a bone-shaking jolt. The wings beat madly again, and they slid through the fronds and settled on the ground below.

"You didn't need to strangle me!" Hathor said reproachfully. "I've been flying for nearly three thousand years and never crashed once."

"I'm sorry," gasped Kandaki. "It's just that it's very new to me." She slid off Hathor's back and picked up her bundle of linens. "Will you wait for me here?" she asked.

Hathor nodded. "I'll hide in the trees, though. Better to stay out of sight." So Kandaki set off, on rather wobbly legs, to buy the goats.

She went to the first house she came to, knocked on the door, and told the farmer's wife who answered that she was with some traders camped "down in the palm grove" and that she wanted to buy some goats. The farmer's wife invited her in, beaming, and exclaimed over the linens with delight. In no time she'd agreed to trade three young goats, some bread, and a jar of beer, for a kilt, a shift, and a cloak, and she called her husband to help carry the things. Kandaki walked out of the house carrying the beer while the farmer's wife carried the bread and the farmer himself led the goats. She'd watched how the farmer's wife carried the beer jug when she brought it from the cellar and was able to put it on her head in just the same way. She felt very pleased with herself.

"From upriver, are you?" asked the farmer as they walked toward the grove. "Do you know anything about the goings-on there?"

"No," said Kandaki, abruptly feeling less pleased. "What's been happening?"

"King Arkamon's been killed, him and all his house," replied the farmer. "They say that he was planning to hand us over to the Egyptians. He'd agreed to make Nubia an Egyptian province, provided he was viceroy."

"I don't believe that!" said the farmer's wife before Kandaki could say anything. "It's just that fellow Shabako, the captain of the royal guard that was, wanting to make himself a king."

"I'm not so sure," said the farmer, shaking his head. "They do say that King Arkamon had been treating with the Egyptians, and no good ever came of that. I remember when they sacked Napata, in my grandfather's day; they carried off all Granddad's sheep on the way down and all his goats on the way back."

"Well, I don't believe King Arkamon would betray

his own people," said the farmer's wife. "He was always a good king. And that Shabako is a cruel, hard man. I heard this morning from Taharka's wife over in Derr that he sent the young princess up there to be eaten by the water dragon. She said the galley arrived this very morning!"

"Well!" exclaimed the farmer. "Well! Mind you, the water dragon is a god, and no good came of banning the worship of it."

"I don't think any good comes of worshiping gods as cruel as it is," replied his wife.

"Why, they're the very gods you have to worship most," returned the farmer. "They're the ones most likely to do something nasty if you don't worship them. Ever since King Arkamon banned sacrifices to it, I've been afraid it would come upstream and eat the goats."

His wife shook her head. "You can say what you like, but *I* won't worship the horrible thing. And no good ever came of killing kings. It makes the gods angry, and it's us that have to suffer for it."

The farmer grunted. Before Kandaki could think of something to say, they'd reached the palm grove. "Where are your friends?" asked the farmer, looking at the shadows under the trees, empty in the dusk.

"Oh, they must be seeing to the donkeys," Kandaki replied, thinking quickly. "Just leave the things here."

He grunted, and he and his wife left. As soon as they were gone, Hathor glided out of the trees like an enormous bat.

The goats saw her and bleated in terror. They turned

and ran. Hathor sailed past Kandaki, landed on the first
goat, killing it with one blow of her talons. She twisted
and leaped with outstretched wings and killed the second, while knocking the third over with her tail. Before
it could get up again, she'd torn its throat open. Then
she rubbed her head against her foreleg and folded her
wings. "I'm glad you succeeded," she said in her soft
voice. "I haven't eaten since yesterday."

"Why should *you* be afraid of *humans*?" asked Kandaki incredulously, looking at the three dead goats. "You
could kill a dozen men in a minute!"

Hathor shook her head. "Men have arrows, and they
have nets," she said sadly. "And there are always so
many more of you than of us. If you have any of the
linen left, tie those goats across my back, will you? I
can't carry you and them both; I'll move them now and
come back."

Kandaki slung the goats over Hathor's back, and the
dragon flew off. The dusk slowly deepened into night.
Kandaki walked back and forth under the trees, thinking
about what the farmer had said. Lies, lies, lies—and
some people believed them, even here, near Derr! How
could she win back her father's throne if people believed
it was her father, and not Shabako, who had turned traitor to Nubia? She blinked at tears and wished she'd succeeded in getting the sword into Shabako.

Hathor returned, a shadow in the darkness, and settled at the foot of the trees. Kandaki slung the bread to
one side of her, the beer to the other, and climbed onto
the dragon's back. They flew back downriver—lower

than before, under the cover of the darkness. The marshes were a patch of velvet black under the stars. Hathor crossed them quickly and glided down on the far side, the desert side, landing neatly beside a low red fire. Baki jumped up, smiling.

"Well done!" he said to Kandaki, helping her off Hathor's back and then collecting the beer. "The meat's cooking. We've already split the bones, and Bad-luck's swimming to that heap of rocks to leave them there. The other things are there already."

"You've moved the *Lucky Lady*," said Kandaki.

"Yes. Bad-luck reckons it's hidden better on this side of the marsh. And we wanted to build a fire. The water thing sank like a rock, by the way, so we're all ready for the morning. And I don't think there's any reason to be afraid."

But the next morning, when the galley nosed slowly into the lake, Kandaki was afraid anyway.

4

How to Kill a Lie

THEY LEFT THE *LUCKY LADY* HIDDEN ON THE
DESERT SIDE OF THE MARSH WHEN DAY
dawned and hid in the reeds beside the lake. Kashta's
galley wasn't long in coming; the sky was still pink
when they heard the cautious splashing of the oars, and
the long boat edged over toward the heap of rocks. They
saw Kashta and the old priest jump down beside the
broken stone column and look at the tangle of muddy
cloth, bone, and gold that lay beside it.

"Well," said Kashta, his voice carrying clearly in the
stillness, "it's had her."

But the priest was patting the broken column much
as the monster had done. "Oh, look!" he cried. "Oh,
what can have happened! Why did it do that?"

"I suppose because it was particularly hungry," said
Kashta impatiently. "Don't worry, old man, King Shabako will pay for a new one."

"But it's never done that before! It must have been
angry. And there was all that smoke and steam coming
from the marsh yesterday. That's never happened before

either. There's something *wrong*, I tell you. I can smell it. The air is different.''

The air was different that morning, too; the strange cold smell was gone, and the marshes were beginning to smell like marshes again, wet and green.

The old priest pulled the shackles out of the hole in the broken column. "The bolts are missing," he said. Prahotep had carefully removed them, so that no one would see they'd been sawed through.

"Probably your god was just excited at getting a sacrifice again, after so long without," said Kashta. "It's had the princess, you can be sure of that. Come on, old man. You can go plan whom to give to it next." He picked up the shreds of bone, the necklace, and a strand of jeweled hair and wrapped them in the scrap of dress. "I'll take these back to King Shabako. It's good-bye forever to the royal house of Arkamon!" And he climbed back into the galley. The old man followed, muttering and shaking his head, and the boat turned, the oars splashed, and Kashta and his crew vanished out the other side of the marsh.

"It's not 'good-bye,' Kashta," Kandaki murmured. "It's 'see you soon.' And when I see you next, you won't be so happy!"

Prahotep let out his breath in a contented sigh. "Well, that's that!" he said. "I'm having a swim before breakfast; anyone want to join me?"

"Swim?" demanded Kandaki impatiently. "Breakfast? Shouldn't we leave at once? Kashta will go back to Derr to drop off the priest; if we hurry, we'll have a good head start on him."

"Then he'd catch us on the river," replied Prahotep. "A galley like that can travel much faster than we can. No, we'll have breakfast and wait for him to get ahead of us. It's safer."

In a few minutes Prahotep and Baki were splashing in the chest-high water around the *Lucky Lady*. Hathor and Kandaki sat on the bank beside the fire and watched. Hathor shuddered delicately.

"Swimming for *pleasure!*" she exclaimed. "I just can't see it. I *hate* getting wet."

"I think it looks like fun," said Kandaki.

"Why don't you join them then?"

Kandaki pulled moodily at her hair. "I can't swim," she said.

When she was growing up, she'd always been told that splashing about in the river was something for servants and workers to do, beneath the dignity of a princess. She'd never minded not knowing how to swim—until now. Now she felt she'd missed out on something. She began to wonder how much else she'd missed out on.

Baki couldn't swim very well; he flailed and splashed and moved slowly. But Prahotep was like a diver duck, vanishing and reappearing suddenly somewhere else. He slid up behind Baki and paused, looked toward Kandaki, and pointed at the swordsman, grinning and making a dunking motion. Kandaki grinned back and nodded.

Prahotep vanished, and a moment later Baki's head dipped under the water. He came up coughing and shouting. Prahotep resurfaced, laughing. Baki splashed him with a great wall of water. Prahotep disappeared again.

In a moment, though, he reappeared. Baki began splashing him again, but Prahotep raised his hand. "Wait a moment!" he shouted. "I've found something."

He waded toward the shore, and Baki, curious now, came after him. Prahotep stopped at the water's edge and examined his find. It was a lump of mud—with a bit of gold glinting in it. "I saw it shining in the reeds when I dived," he explained. "Let me see. . . ."

He stooped and rinsed it in the water. The mud washed off in lumps, showing a kind of wide gold bracelet with a hooked projection on one side.

"It's an archer's wrist guard," said Kandaki, coming down to look at it. "But what a magnificent one! I wonder how it got there?" It was decorated with an eye, picked out in blue lapis lazuli, and there were hieroglyphics carved into the band.

Prahotep offered it to her. "Can you read what it says, Princess?"

"Me? No, I'm no scribe." She took the wrist guard and turned it back and forth. "That's the sign of the god Apedemek, though, the lion god, patron of the royal house. I recognize that. I wonder if this belonged to some brave warrior of my father's, who came here to kill the water dragon?" She imagined him meeting the monster and shuddered. She handed the wrist guard back.

Hathor had also come over; she sniffed at the wrist guard, and her tongue flickered. "This is too old to have belonged to one of your father's men," she declared. "There's a smell of centuries on it—and a smell of magic, too."

"Magic?" asked Prahotep in alarm. "Maybe we'd better put it back. Or will it turn to lead when you touch it?"

"Oh, it wasn't *made* by magic," Hathor replied. "It isn't that sort of smell; that sorcery stink tipped over whatever's underneath. It's honest gold. But it's been *used* in magic, and strong magic, too, for the smell to last this long. I won't touch it, just in case."

"Do magical things turn to lead when you touch them?" asked Kandaki in surprise.

"Only if they were made of lead to begin with," replied the dragon. "Spells don't work on dragons. Anything made by human magic would turn back into what it really is if I touched it. I don't think there's any harm in that thing now, Prahotep, and it's very pretty. If I'd found it, I'd keep it. Why don't you keep it?"

"Very well," he said, pleased. He put it on his arm; it was too big. He took it off again and put it in the boat. "I wish I knew how to shoot," he said, patting it. "Then I could use it. Let's have breakfast."

When they'd eaten, they set out again across the marsh. A flock of ducks had landed on the black lake, and a small bird had flown into the reeds and begun singing. A dragonfly hawked, brilliantly blue, before the boat. "This place is coming to life!" Kandaki exclaimed with delight.

"I think that old man will guess what's happened before long," said Prahotep, "but by then we'll be far away."

Just before they reached the Nile, Hathor jumped out of the boat and began flying upward. Baki and Prahotep stopped rowing for a moment and waved, then went back to their oars. The dragon climbed upward until she was almost invisible against the sky. "She does that every day," Baki explained. "She hates being cramped in the cabin, and it's very useful for us. She can see if anyone's coming and give warning."

At the river Prahotep raised the *Lucky Lady*'s sail, and the boat jumped joyfully under the north breeze and began running sweetly upstream. There was no more need to row, and Baki went forward to sit in the bow, while Prahotep steered. Kandaki sat down at the foot of the mast, scowling. She was again remembering what the farmer had said about her father.

"What's the matter?" Baki asked her.

She told him. "It's so unfair!" she finished. "Father was only negotiating a treaty on trade. Nubians have been going downriver to trade with Egypt for generations, and he wanted to arrange things like how much customs duty they should pay and what would happen to them if they got into trouble; he wanted to help them and protect them. But now plenty of people are going to believe he meant to betray all Nubia, and that means they'll support Shabako. When I call on my father's friends to help me against Shabako, they'll murmur this foul lie about my father and suspect me! You can kill a man, but how can you kill a lie?"

"I don't know," said Baki. "I've never thought of that. Of course"—he looked embarrassed—"I've always thought it would be a good thing if Nubia were an Egyptian province. After all, northern Nubia has been one for centuries. But I can see you view things very differently here in the south, and I suppose I'll have to learn to see things your way. Will this man we're going to see in Napata believe Shabako's lie?"

"Uncle Mandu? Never. He knows my fa—knew my father very well. He knows my father never betrayed anyone in all his life." Kandaki wiped her eyes angrily, remembering Mandulis laughing with her mother and father in Meroë. I never even had much time with them, she thought miserably; they were always so busy ruling. And now I never will have time. "No, but people who didn't know my father well will believe it. My father kept the peace with Egypt for his whole reign, for twenty years, and people will start saying he was weak and cowardly because he spared them a war!"

Baki made a sympathetic noise. "I know what it's like to be lied about," he said. "When I was in Pharaoh's army, my captain used to call me weak and cowardly because I treated the convicts we were guarding like men instead of beating them like donkeys."

"That was Kenna?" asked Prahotep, looking up from his seat in the stern.

Baki nodded. "And we'd both of us be killed for a lie if we went back to Egypt," he said to his friend. "I imagine we're still wanted for robbing the temple of Anubis in Thebes."

"That's why you're wanted in Egypt?" asked Kandaki, shocked. "You robbed a temple?"

"No—I mean, yes," Baki replied awkwardly. "We're wanted for robbing a temple, but we didn't. But Nefersenet said we'd done it, to get us arrested, and because he was priest of Anubis, everyone believed it."

"Who's Nefersenet?"

"He was a magician," said Prahotep, looking uncomfortable at the thought.

"He wanted to bathe in dragon's blood," Baki put in.

Prahotep nodded. "He thought he'd live ten thousand years if he did that, though Hathor says he wouldn't do any such thing."

"He thought he would, though," continued Baki, "so he wanted a dragon. And he was a very powerful and important man. He found out about Hathor when Bad-luck sold some of her treasure to pay for the *Lucky Lady,* and he did everything he could to get hold of her. He came after us himself from Thebes to the Belly of Stones. As Amun lives, I thought we'd never reach Nubia."

"What happened to him?" asked Kandaki, impressed.

The two men looked at each other. "He's dead," said Baki. "He caught us in the end, and we killed him defending ourselves. We left him buried under the figurehead of his boat, in the center of the Belly of Stones."

There was a sudden rush of wings, and Hathor landed on the boat, making it rock wildly. "That galley is on the bend just behind us!" she cried.

"What!" exclaimed Prahotep, jumping to his feet. "I thought it was going upriver in front of us!"

"It must have stayed longer in Derr," said the dragon, very distressed. "I'm sorry—I wasn't looking out for it, I was over the desert, trying to see if there was much game, and now it's almost on top of us!"

Prahotep glanced about quickly. The banks of the river were open, bordered by wheat fields. "What's ahead?" he asked Hathor anxiously.

"A village!" moaned the dragon. "There's nowhere to hide!"

"Princess," Prahotep said hurriedly, "would they recognize this boat as Egyptian? If we went over to the other side of the river, I mean, where they couldn't see that Baki and I aren't quite as dark as proper Nubians?"

Kandaki bit her lip. "*I* recognized the boat as Egyptian," she said, "and I don't know anything about boats. Of course, there are plenty of Egyptian-built boats in Nubia, since traders buy them sometimes, and, if it comes to that, there are plenty of Nubians as light-skinned as you, at least here in the north. But—but I think Kashta will check on us as soon as he sees us, and you don't speak Nubian. He's second-in-command to Shabako, and he'll understand perfectly how useful it would be to have a couple of Egyptians to accuse of spying."

Prahotep's face went perfectly blank. Baki loosened his sword. "How many men are there on the boat?" he asked grimly.

"Thirty-two, including Kashta and the captain," Kandaki told him. "And at least half of them are armed with bows."

Baki swore. "Too many. Fifteen, even twenty we might manage, with Hathor's help, but not more. And against arrows—"

He stopped. Prahotep's face had lit in a sudden smile.

"You have an idea!" exclaimed Baki.

Prahotep nodded. "Princess, does Kashta speak Egyptian?"

"Yes," replied Kandaki, taken aback. "Most important Nubians do. But—"

Prahotep grinned. It was a nervous grin, with a lot of teeth, but a grin nonetheless. "Hathor, Princess, you two go hide in the cabin. Toss me the lion skin. Baki, we're going to turn the boat around."

"And go straight toward them?"

"Yes. What you and the princess were saying just now—I know how to kill a lie. I just hope it works!"

Kandaki backed hurriedly into the *Lucky Lady*'s tiny rush-covered cabin. It was full of treasure and very cramped, and she had to sit on Hathor's tail. The lion skin was wedged into a treasure box; she pulled it out and tossed it to Prahotep, who put it on. Then he turned the boat around, heading back downsteam the way they'd come.

Kandaki poked a finger through the rushes and peered tensely at the river. In a few minutes she saw Kashta's galley rounding the bend, its oars flashing in the sunlight. The *Lucky Lady* drifted down the current toward it, and she saw the oars slow their beat as someone on the galley noticed the Egyptian lines of the sailing barge.

"Steer close to them," Prahotep told Baki. "I'll do the talking."

When the *Lucky Lady* was only a stone's throw from Kashta's galley, Prahotep ran into the bow. Kandaki could see the archers lining the side of the galley now, their bows strung and arrows at the ready. But Prahotep paid no attention to them. "Ahoy there!" he shouted. "Is this vessel commanded by a man called Kashta?"

There was a stir, and then Kashta's face appeared among the archers. "Who asks for me in Egyptian?" he demanded angrily. "What are you doing on this river, foreigner?"

"Talking to you, if you're Kashta," replied Prahotep. "Stop for a minute and throw us a line, will you?"

Someone on the galley tossed a rope to the *Lucky Lady*. Baki caught it and made it fast to the stern. Someone else tossed a hook anchor, which caught and held the two boats in midstream. Prahotep scrambled up the galley's side to her deck and straightened his lion skin. Kandaki, craning her neck to see, held her breath. Kashta was a tall man. He stood in the middle of the deck, wearing a leopard skin over his shoulders, armed with a bright sword, and he was glowering savagely. The Egyptian looked very small in front of him.

"Very good," Prahotep said, smiling. "I'm Nefersenet of Thebes. I expect your master Shabako's told you about me. He said you'd be in this part of the river if I needed to send him a message."

Kashta's glower turned to a look of consternation. "You've come from King Shabako?" he asked.

"Yes—about the arrangements. You know. Tell him I've reconsidered his terms, and I don't think they're so unreasonable after all. I've thought of a good way to put them to my master, the Beloved of Amun, and I think I can say that the Lord of the Two Lands will probably accept. And thank him for me for his hospitality."

"The Beloved of Amun?" repeated Kashta in bewilderment. "The Lord of the Two Lands? You mean, the pharaoh of Egypt?"

"Of course—life and prosperity to him!" Prahotep raised his hands and bowed slightly in the usual Egyptian reverence. "Shabako told you I was high in his councils, didn't he?"

"No," replied Kashta, stunned.

"Oh, well! Yes, I am Fan Bearer on the Left Side of Pharaoh, and chief priest of Thoth, of Anubis, and of Horus. I am a man who can speak for the Lord of the Two Lands with some authority. And as you see, Shabako has honored me with the royal lion skin. Now, do you have my message, or shall I repeat it?"

"Shabako's been negotiating with the pharaoh of Egypt?" Kashta demanded, thunderstruck.

"Didn't he *tell* you?" asked Prahotep. "I assumed—as I love life, I thought you were his second-in-command and high in his confidence! This is awkward."

"What has Shabako been arranging with Pharaoh?" Kashta asked in anguish. "We murdered Arkamon for making arrangements with Pharaoh; what has Shabako arranged?"

"If King Shabako hasn't told you, I hardly think I should," replied Prahotep. "This is very awkward. I assumed that you knew already. Well, give my apologies to King Shabako if I've spoken out of turn. Don't worry, I'm sure the king will be able to explain everything to you, my friend. Do you have my message, or shall I repeat it?"

"Repeat it," said Kashta grimly.

Prahotep carefully repeated it, then glanced about the galley. "A very fine vessel," he said cheerfully, "and I'd love to stay aboard and sample your hospitality. You can see I've had to use just a small craft, for the sake of secrecy, and I'm sure it's not as comfortable as this one. But the affair is urgent, and your master urged me to make haste. Good-bye, Lord Kashta. I hope when we next meet, we'll have more time." He began to climb back down into the *Lucky Lady*.

"Lord Kashta!" cried the captain of the galley in Nubian. "Should I stop him?"

Kashta, looking like a man who'd walked into a wall, was watching Prahotep from the bow. "No," he said.

Prahotep jumped back into the sailing barge and signaled Baki to untie her.

One of the archers on the galley pulled nervously at his bow. "But you said we should stop any Egyptians we met on the river!" complained the galley's captain.

Kashta turned to him furiously. "Don't you understand Egyptian, you stupid dog? He said he'd come from King Shabako!"

Baki had loosened the rope, and the *Lady* drifted back into the current. "Was he telling the truth?" asked the captain.

"He wouldn't have made right for us and asked for me by name if he weren't, would he?" snapped Kashta. "Put those bows down, you men, and get back to your oars!"

Baki straightened the *Lady* with the steering oar, and Prahotep waved cheerfully to Kashta as the boat swept on downriver and around the bend.

When the galley had disappeared, Prahotep sat down heavily, wiped his eyes, and started shaking. For a moment Kandaki thought he was laughing. Then she saw his face.

"As I love life and hate death," he said, "I was so frightened I thought I was going to be sick!"

"You didn't sound it," said Kandaki.

"That's because I was so frightened I was babbling," he replied. "But anyhow, it seems to have worked."

"I don't understand it," Hathor said. "These human plots are too full of lies for me to follow. How did it work?"

Baki let out a whoop of laughter. "Kashta obviously hates Egypt and knows his master well enough not to trust him. Now he believes that Shabako has been negotiating with Pharaoh behind his back. He wouldn't touch us because we're friends of Shabako, but I'll bet he'll have a few things to say to his master when he gets back to Meroë!"

"I hope he'll have a few things to say to his friends on the way upriver as well," said Prahotep. "The more the story spreads, the better."

"So you think that this story of yours might spread," Kandaki asked Prahotep, "that people will believe that Shabako is negotiating with Egypt?"

Prahotep nodded.

"And if they believe Shabako is, then they'll believe my father wasn't!"

"That's how you kill a lie," said Prahotep. "You tell another one—only bigger!"

5
Napata

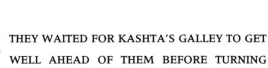

THEY WAITED FOR KASHTA'S GALLEY TO GET WELL AHEAD OF THEM BEFORE TURNING the *Lucky Lady* and sailing upstream again. Hathor took to the sky, promising soberly to keep a sharp watch on the river this time and warn them sooner of any trouble ahead.

"And if we meet anyone else who questions us," Prahotep said, "you can do the talking, Princess, and pretend we're all Nubians. You can say that Baki and I are just a couple of northerners, going south to trade the linen. But I think you should start teaching us the language, just in case."

Kandaki was silent for a minute. "I'll teach you both to speak Nubian on one condition," she replied at last. "You each have to teach me something in return."

Baki looked puzzled, and Prahotep looked shocked. "I don't think either of us knows anything proper to royalty, Princess," he told her.

"I don't care if it's *proper*," said Kandaki. "You can teach me to swim. And Baki can teach me how to fight with a sword and—do you know how to shoot?"

"Of course," said Baki, but now he looked shocked, too. "But fighting's not something any girl should learn, let alone a princess."

"I'm not any girl," Kandaki replied. "I'm going to have to lead my people in a war and I want to know how to defend myself. And I don't want to have to hide in the cabin if we meet Kashta again!"

Baki whistled. "I can see why a lion god is patron of your house!" he exclaimed. "You have the spirit of a lioness! Very well, I'll teach you how to defend yourself."

But Prahotep looked embarrassed. "I don't think it's right for a princess to splash about in the water like a fisherman," he muttered.

"You do!" snapped Kandaki.

"Yes, but I am!"

"You can't be anything . . . lowborn like that," Kandaki told him. "You're too clever."

"But I am a fisherman!" Prahotep protested. "What's more, I'm a thief. I used to steal vegetables from other people's gardens. And once I almost robbed a tomb. I'm very lowborn and unimportant. It's not right for me to teach a great lady anything."

"You're lying to me, like you did to Kashta," said Kandaki. "You just have some reason you don't *want* to teach me." She pulled angrily at her hair.

Baki laughed. "They said before that you were a magician, Bad-luck, because you couldn't have got the better of one otherwise. Now, it seems, you must be a nobleman, or you couldn't have outwitted one. Teach the princess swimming if she wants to learn. If anyone objects, you can always say that it's what the great lady ordered, and a thief and fisherman like you had no choice but to obey."

"I knew you were lying," said Kandaki.

For the first time since she'd met him, Prahotep looked angry. "I wouldn't lie to you, Princess!" he said sharply. "I was a fisherman, and if I hadn't had such bad luck at it, I still would be. And you, Baki—it's not fair for you to laugh at me, too, just because you're a soldier and more nobly born than I am!"

Baki stopped grinning. "I'm sorry," he said, puzzled. "I wasn't laughing at you, Bad-luck. Not the way you mean, anyway."

Prahotep said nothing. He stared sullenly upstream, watching the river.

"I'll teach you Nubian, anyway," said Kandaki after a long silence.

At that he looked back at her, and the sullen, angry expression slowly faded from his eyes. "How do you say, 'The boat sails upriver,' then?" he asked, and she told him.

In the evening they moored the *Lucky Lady* beside a vineyard, and Kandaki gave some linens to the vineyard's owner in exchange for two sheep, some flour, and some grapes. They cooked a leg of mutton and some flatbread on a fire made of driftwood, while Hathor lay curled under the vines, tearing the rest of the sheep into strips and swallowing them. The stars began to come out, white and huge in the velvet dusk.

"The boat sails upriver," said Prahotep in Nubian. "Today the boat rowed downriver. Tomorrow the boat will sail. She will sail upriver with the wind." He grinned.

"Show-off," said Baki. He began to eat some grapes.

"You ought to have paid more attention," said Prahotep, in Egyptian again.

"*I* don't remember something someone's told me only once! At this rate, you'll owe the princess three swimming lessons for every one fighting lesson she gets from me."

"I haven't had any lessons yet," said Kandaki, "and I've been teaching all day. Get up, Baki, and show me how to hold a sword! I'll see if I can buy one for myself and some bows for all of us tomorrow."

Baki showed her how to hold a sword. And in the morning, much to her surprise and delight, Prahotep offered to teach her swimming, just as though he'd never refused.

They sailed up the river for another eight days, going slowly against the current. Kandaki was impatient. "Can't we go faster?" she asked. "The gods know what Shabako may be doing to my father's supporters! Can't you row at least some of the time?"

"There's no sense in rowing upriver, not with only three of us to man the oars," returned Prahotep. "We'd go no faster than we do now with just the wind. If anything, it would slow us down."

"Can't we sail until later, then? If we sailed for even a couple of hours during the night—"

At this both men shook their heads. "We can't sail

at night," said Baki. "I learned that back in Egypt. The river has shallows where a boat like the *Lady* can run aground. We don't know where they are, and we can't avoid them in the dark."

Kandaki bit her lip.

"We're making better speed than you think," Prahotep told her comfortingly. "The *Lady*'s a sweet sailer. Even a galley couldn't do much better than we can against this current."

So they continued to sail peacefully south during the day, camping as soon as the light failed. Kandaki bought supplies and spoke Nubian to the boats they passed. They had no trouble from any enemies, but the farmers and boats were full of news, nearly all of it bad. Many of the most loyal nobles had been at the court in Meroë when Shabako turned traitor, and they were now imprisoned in the palace. Their followers were afraid to move in case Shabako killed them. Many of the cities of Nubia had sworn loyalty to Shabako and were sending troops to fight against a rumored invasion by Egypt. Shabako was marching north at the head of an army that was growing bigger by the day, and no one would stand against him.

"It doesn't sound very promising, Princess," Baki said unhappily. "Are you sure you want to go on? You could always hide for a bit and start an uprising when Shabako's army has gone back to work in the fields."

"I won't run away," she answered, "and if I wait, Shabako may execute his prisoners or start that war with Egypt."

And after a few days Kandaki heard one piece of news that cheered her. "They say that Shabako will never use his army against Egypt," a date grower told her as she was buying supplies one evening. "They say he's in the pay of Pharaoh himself! He's been meeting with a priest called Nefersenet, from Thebes, a man they say is a powerful magician and one of Pharaoh's favorites. They say it's all lies about King Arkamon negotiating with Egypt."

"What do you think?" asked Kandaki.

The date grower shook his head. "I don't know what to think anymore. I'm in no hurry to fight for Shabako, I can tell you that, sister, nor are the other fellows in the region. But he wants to be king, and who wants to stop him? Wait and see, that's what I say."

"*I* want to stop him," Kandaki whispered to herself as she walked back to the boat. "I *must* stop him. I *will* stop him. O gods, help me stop him, please!" She walked on, carrying the basket of bread and dates and leading a reluctant sheep, imagining battles against Shabako. She'd never seen a battle, and as she pictured the swords, the arrows, the blood, she started to feel afraid. She walked faster and faster, until she was almost running, and the sheep bleated angrily and jerked against the rope, and she wasn't sure whether she was running toward her imaginary battle or away from it. Then she rounded a grove of date palms and saw the *Lucky Lady*, and the men sitting by the fire, and the dragon curled up behind them with her head resting on the tip of her tail, and suddenly everything was all right again. The gods had helped her once already; they had sent her friends. That evening she wanted a lesson in fighting even before they'd had supper.

There was a fighting lesson every evening, and a swimming lesson every morning, and Nubian lessons all day. At the end of that time Prahotep spoke a bit of Nubian, Baki a very little of it, and Kandaki could paddle the length of the *Lucky Lady*, hold a sword enough to defend herself, and draw a bow.

Baki also profited by the lessons to improve his swimming and tried to teach Prahotep how to fight, but without much success. Prahotep would take a sword or bow only reluctantly and dropped it very quickly when anything went wrong.

"You're not trying!" complained Baki. "Kandaki doesn't know any more about it than you, but she tries! She doesn't keep pushing *after* her blade's been parried."

"The princess comes from a house of warrior kings," Prahotep said sullenly. "I don't."

"Oh, be quiet!" ordered Baki irritably. "You never used to worry about that. What's got into you? Don't you want to learn how to fight?"

"No," Prahotep answered shortly. And most evenings he wouldn't even touch the swords but sat beside Hathor and watched while Baki and Kandaki fenced or shot.

But apart from that, the journey was peaceful, so peaceful and so pleasant that Kandaki sometimes found it hard to remember that she was a princess sailing to her father's foremost general to begin a war, not a merchant's daughter traveling for fun. After the first five days the land grew greener, and Hathor reported that there were occasional water holes in the desert beyond the river and that game was more plentiful. She began to return to the boat in the evenings with an antelope or a wild goat for their supper, and Kandaki was relieved. The cost of two sheep a day was exhausting the supply of linen rather quickly.

On the evening of the eighth day Kandaki learned in the village where she bought bread that the city of Napata was only a few hours' sailing ahead.

"And I wouldn't go that way, sister," the baker told her. "Shabako, the new king, has arrived at the city with all his army and surrounded it. He hasn't actually besieged it yet—people are still allowed in and out—but who knows what might happen tomorrow? King Shabako wants Lord Mandulis, our governor, to swear loyalty to him. Lord Mandulis says he'll never swear loyalty to the man who killed King Arkamon, but what he'll do instead, no one knows. Some say that he's going to retire peacefully to Egypt, but I don't believe that. If any of the royal house were left alive, he'd proclaim them rightful rulers of Nubia and fight for them, but they're all gone—except for the Princess Abar, the old king's niece, and she's married Shabako. Maybe he'll make himself king. Then there'll be a fierce battle! Whatever he decides, a girl like you ought to stay well clear of it."

Kandaki thanked the baker and went back to the *Lucky Lady*, where she told the others about it. "I knew

I could trust Uncle Mandu!" she finished happily. "Now all we have to do is get into Napata, and we'll be safe with our friends."

Prahotep looked at the ground and said nothing. Baki looked uncertain. "All we have to do is get into Napata!" he exclaimed. "That might not be so easy, with Shabako's army surrounding it. Just because they're letting Nubians in and out doesn't mean they'll let us. If we go on in the *Lucky Lady*, we'll probably find a dozen war galleys on our tail, and if they catch us, it's the end."

Kandaki looked at Prahotep expectantly. When he still said nothing, she said, "We can get around that, can't we? We could hide the boat and go in on foot—or Hathor could fly us in at night, one by one."

At that Prahotep did look up. "I don't think Hathor should go into the city at all!" he said angrily. "We'll be safe with our friends, you said. But they're not *our* friends; they're *your* friends. This Mandulis doesn't know us—and he won't want to, either. With all the rumors of secret negotiations with Egypt, the last thing he'll want is a couple of Egyptians slipping into the city by night. His enemies will accuse him—and you—of being in Pharaoh's pay! As for Hathor, for all he knows, she's the water dragon of Derr. It wouldn't be much use for him to say he's sorry afterward if he shoots her full of arrows the moment she appears. Hathor, do you want to go into the city?"

"No," said the dragon firmly. "I said from the start that I wouldn't get involved in human wars. We agreed

to help the princess as far as Napata, and if we can think
of a way for her to go into the city safely, I think we'll
have kept our bargain.''

Kandaki bit her lip. She hadn't realized how much
she'd relied on the Egyptians' coming with her.

''But—but,'' protested Baki, ''Bad-luck, you said we
were on the side of Princess Kandaki, and as Amun
lives, that's true! If we stay with the princess, we'll have
her friends to protect us and to help us when the war is
over. But wandering into the middle of a land at war,
where any Egyptian is likely to be arrested or killed by
anyone—that's insane! You can think of *some* way to get
us all into the city safely, can't you?''

''No!'' snapped Prahotep. ''I told you, I don't think
Hathor should go into the city at all. Princess Kandaki
can get in on her own easily. The city isn't actually besieged yet, and there'd be no reason for anyone to stop
a Nubian. It's only Egyptians like us who have to be
afraid; if we came down, we'd only put her in danger. I
think we should hide the boat and the treasure somewhere and strike off overland to look for dragons. The
princess can reward us when the war is over, if she wins
it and still remembers us.''

''If!'' cried Kandaki furiously. ''Do you think I'd for-
get the people I owe my life to?''

''As Amun lives!'' Baki said under his breath. ''Bad-
luck, I can't believe I've seen something you haven't, but
don't you understand what this could mean? If we go
into the city with the princess, we'll have a part to play
in fighting this Shabako, and, from the sound of him,

I'm happy to fight him with all my strength. It'll be a
dark day for Nubia if he wins, and not such a bright one
for Egypt, either. And if we defeat him, we'll be the
friends and helpers of a queen! We'll be rich and important men, more than we ever dreamed was possible.
But if we don't stay with the princess now, though she
can still make us rich, she won't be able to make us
important. Other men, who've fought in the war, will
have places that might have been ours, and she won't
be able to steal those places back for us. This is the sort
of chance one man in a thousand is offered once in a
lifetime. You can't throw it away!"

Prahotep was silent for a minute, blinking. "*You*
can't throw it away," he said heavily. "I see that. Well,
you agreed to come to Nubia because I asked you to,
because I wanted help with the boat. Hathor promised
you whatever piece of her treasure you liked most. Very
well, we're here, and we're about to leave the boat. Take
your piece of the treasure, and go on into the city with
the princess. I'll stay with Hathor."

Baki's mouth dropped. "You can't say that!"

"Baki, you know I didn't come here to overthrow
Shabako or even to help Kandaki. I came to look for dragons with Hathor. And that's more important. Kings and
queens come and go, the best and the worst of them. Shabako will die, and someone else will replace him, whatever we do. And Kandaki has friends, rich and important
friends, who'll be eager to help her now. I won't be
missed. But Hathor is one of the last dragons, perhaps the
very last, and there's no one to help her but me. If she is

gone, a whole kind is gone, a wonder that can never be replaced, not by any king, not by the gods themselves. May I die and lie unburied before I see that happen!"

"I would miss you," Kandaki said. She stared at him, but he did not answer and wouldn't meet her eyes.

Hathor looked at him as well, then leaned over and licked his cheek. "Prahotep," she said gently, "I don't need you to come with me. If we're going to hide the boat and go overland, I'd do just as well flying by myself. Go into the city with Baki and Kandaki. Take some of my treasure with you, as your own. We can arrange a place to meet in a year or so, and I can collect the rest of the treasure then."

Prahotep put his arms about her neck. "I don't want any of your treasure," he told her. "You need a human to help you. You need someone to ask directions to where the dragons are supposed to be and to buy sheep for you if the hunting's bad. As I love life and hate death, if anything happened to you that I could have prevented, even if I became the richest man in Nubia, I'd still consider myself wretched and my life a waste."

"Very well then," Hathor said, "and—thank you. You and I will go overland, and Baki and Kandaki will go into the city." She licked his cheek again.

Kandaki got to her feet. She felt at once furious, sad, and ashamed. But she could see that it was no use trying to argue. "Prahotep," she said, "can you think of a way to get Baki into the city at least?"

He shook his head. "You don't need me for that. If you walk in on your own first, you can arrange it yourself."

She glared at him. He still wouldn't meet her eyes. "I suppose I could walk in like a country woman going to market," she said at last. "I could carry a basket of fruit or something. Then, when I've met my friends, I could tell someone to meet Baki somewhere we've arranged beforehand, and they could bring him in."

"Hathor can fly over the city, high up," said Baki, "and see if there are any likely places for me to wait."

"I could find a good place to leave the *Lucky Lady*, too," agreed Hathor.

"Thank you. And could you and Prahotep wait with Baki?" Kandaki tried hard to keep the anger out of her voice. The last thing she wanted to do was quarrel with Prahotep now. "Then I could send you some goods to trade, and food and some donkeys to carry it all, to help you on your journey. You'd have a hard time buying enough sheep with what you could carry going on foot, and you'd be very short of water."

"Oh!" said Prahotep, brightening a very little. "Yes, please. Thank you. But only one donkey, please: I'm not very skilled with them."

The following morning they set off in the *Lucky Lady* for the last time. Hathor rose quickly into the clear sky until she was an almost-invisible fleck against the blue, then glided off upriver. She returned little more than an hour later. "There's an old canal leading from the river on the west bank a little way ahead," she said. "It runs through some fields and ends in a clump of scrub and papyrus. I think it's probably a good place to leave the boat, though I'll have to find somewhere else to hide my treasure. It would also be a perfect place for Baki to wait because the canal continues as a dry ditch right up to the city walls. Shabako's men only have one encampment here on the north of Napata, and that's not near the ditch. You could move a whole troop along it and not be noticed."

So they sailed on until they came to the canal and then turned into it.

It wasn't one of the ordinary ditches used for irrigation, but a proper canal built for ships. Kandaki guessed it must have belonged to some rich man of Napata who liked to take his boats onto the river by a private channel. It ran diagonally from the river, and as they followed it, they suddenly saw the city of Napata, still distant, but closer than they'd guessed. Its mud-brick walls towered above the low-lying fields, and its towers were bright with banners. Shortly after they first saw it, the canal ended, as Hathor had said, its stone sides broken down and the water it carried seeping out into a papyrus swamp rimmed with thorny scrub. Probably, thought Kandaki, it had been broken when the Egyptians sacked Napata. Prahotep moored the boat in the thick of the reeds, half grounding it, and they all got out and waded ashore—except Hathor, who flew, landed, and waited for them. Then they stood still and looked at one another.

"I'll go into the city now, then," said Kandaki. "I'll try to come back at nightfall."

"Be careful!" said Prahotep anxiously. "You can probably buy a basket of fruit at any farm around here, and when you've bought it, put it on your head and walk slowly. If you hurry, Shabako's men might notice you. Just send us a message tonight, to let us know you've arrived safely. You don't need to come yourself."

"Yes, I do," replied Kandaki. "I want to say good-bye." She kissed him on the cheek, then hugged both Baki and Hathor and set out toward the walls of Napata.

Not far from the swamp, the old canal went under a road, and Kandaki left one and joined the other. She had walked only a little farther when she found a fat old woman sitting under a date palm with a basket of grapes and lotus seed for sale. The old woman was delighted to sell the basket and everything in it for a few of the gold beads Kandaki had once worn on her hair, and Kandaki put the basket on her head and walked on. It was a surprise to remember that a week before she wouldn't have known how to carry a basket properly.

The northern camp of Shabako's army, which Hathor had mentioned, was directly on the road that led to the gate. Kandaki trudged toward it steadily, bowing her head as though the load were tiring her and letting her hair hang over her face. Her heart thundered, and her palms were slippery with sweat; but no one seemed even to notice her. She passed the first tents and kept walking—slowly. It seemed to take hours.

"Hey!" called a voice behind her. "You there!"

Kandaki stopped. She wanted to throw down the basket and run, but instead she stood still, wondering what Prahotep would think of to say in such a situation.

One of Shabako's men trotted up beside her. "How much are the grapes?" he asked.

Kandaki felt weak with relief. "I'll sell you a big bunch for an egg, sir," she replied.

"I don't have any eggs, sister. I'll give you a kiss, instead."

"That's not worth one grape, let alone a bunch!" she snapped. She realized she would have to bargain, or the man would get suspicious. "You can have it for a copper ring."

"A copper ring for a bunch of grapes! Do you think I'm a fool? Here, wait a minute." He fumbled at his belt and brought out a bead of blue-glazed pottery, the kind poor girls strung in their hair. "What about that?" he asked.

"Very well," said Kandaki. She took the bead, put down the basket, and broke off a bunch of grapes.

"Oh, a few more than that, sister!" complained the soldier. He reached out for another bunch. Kandaki slapped his wrist.

"That's a bead's worth," she told him, "but I'll give you just a little extra, out of the goodness of my heart."

She handed him another four, and he ate them on the spot, grinning at her. "Good fortune to you in the city, sister!" he said.

"Thank you," she answered, and continued through the camp, up to the gates of Napata.

The gates were closed. She walked right up until the massive wooden beams studded with bronze nails towered above her. Then she stopped, looking up as far as she could without tipping over the basket. She saw one of the guards on the gate tower looking down at her.

"The market's closed, girl!" he shouted. "Sorry

you've had the walk for nothing, but the gates are to stay locked in the afternoon, on Lord Mandulis's orders!''

She took the basket off her head and put it down. ''Where is Lord Mandulis?'' she asked, her voice cracking a little.

The guard laughed. ''Hey!'' he called to his fellows. ''There's a country girl here that wants to know where Lord Mandulis is! What are you going to do, sister, complain to him because you can't sell your grapes?''

''Let me in!'' Kandaki called back, beginning to be angry. ''They're not my grapes; I only bought them to give me an excuse to come up to the city. I need to see Lord Mandulis. He'll want to see me—believe me, he will!''

''I'm sure he will . . .'' began the first guard, jokingly, but another man, who wore the leopard skin cloak of an officer, appeared beside him.

''Be quiet,'' he told the first. ''She may have seen something useful in Shabako's army. Why do you want to see Lord Mandulis, girl?''

''Let me in!'' Kandaki called again, glancing nervously behind her. Some of Shabako's soldiers had started toward her.

The officer saw them, too. He nodded to his man, and a moment later the great gate cracked open. Kandaki slipped through, leaving the basket of fruit outside, and the gate banged shut behind her. The guard bolted it, and the officer came down the mud-brick stairway from the tower to stand before her, ''Now,'' he said, ''why do you want to see Lord Mandulis?''

Kandaki felt hot, but she was shivering. She felt horribly drab, a muddy peasant about to claim the royal throne. "Where is he?" she whispered.

The officer raised his eyebrows and grinned. "Why, he was just touring the walls and inspecting the gates. He's coming this way now. He's there!" He nodded toward the walkway that went along the top of the wall, and there, sure enough, was a whole pack of leopard skin cloaks, along with fan bearers and gold-bound spears, and, in the middle of it, a tall man whose white woolly head stood out above the others.

"Uncle Mandu!" shouted Kandaki, and ran up the steps toward him.

The officer from the gate gave a shout; some of the gold-bound spears dropped threateningly, but Lord Mandulis of Napata shoved them aside, a look of joy and amazement lighting up his whole face.

"Kandaki!" he roared, running to her. "Kandaki! My little princess! You're alive!" And he caught her in his arms and hugged her.

Then he fell back a step and dropped to his knees in front of her. He glared at his astonished officers. "Bow, you idiots!" he shouted. "This is Kandaki, daughter of Arkamon, the rightful queen of Nubia!"

6

Dangerous People

AFTER THAT EVERYTHING SEEMED TO HAP-
PEN VERY FAST. EVERYONE BOWED AND
cheered, and Uncle Mandu swept her off to his palace,
where there was more bowing and cheering. Then
Mandu's wife, Amana, appeared. A large plump woman
in a billowing white gown, she shrieked when she saw
Kandaki, then hugged her. "My poor dear girl," cried
Amana, "thank the gods you're alive!"

"Yes, thank the gods, indeed," said Mandulis.
"Amana, we need to get her looking like a queen again
as soon as possible. I want her to appear at the temple
of Amun and Apedemek before evening, to thank the
gods for her safety. Then everyone in the city will be
able to see her and know that it's true, we have a queen
again in Nubia."

"I have some friends who . . ." began Kandaki.

Mandu grinned and kissed her on the cheek. "Tell
me after you've had a bath," he ordered. "Amana,
you're in charge."

A few minutes later, when Kandaki had washed and
put on a clean dress and new jewelry and was sitting

down to let Amana string a new set of green and gold beads on her hair, Mandulis appeared in the doorway.

He beamed at her and sat down on the floor at her feet. "The gods have granted us a miracle," he said. "I've been stalling Shabako with promises for three days now, telling him I might go to Egypt, telling him I might surrender, and all the time trying to find a way to raise the country against him—and you walk up to my gates with a basket of grapes! However did you do it? They said you'd been eaten by the water dragon of Derr."

"When Kashta left me in the marshes of Derr, I met some Egyptians who were hiding there. They killed the water dragon and brought me almost to the city."

Amana stopped stringing beads, staring, and Mandulis whistled. "They killed the water dragon? They say that even the hero Userr, the founder of your house, died trying to slay it. Are you sure it's dead?"

"Yes," Kandaki answered evenly. And she told Mandulis all about the *Lucky Lady* and the three on it and their voyage up the Nile to Napata.

Mandulis whistled again and shook his head. "Clever!" he commented. "Very clever! That story your friend told Kashta is all over the country. Kashta publicly accused Shabako of selling Nubia to the Egyptians, and even though Shabako managed to pacify him, he's still suspicious, and so are a lot of other people. It's been worth half my army, that little story. But these new friends of yours sound dangerous, Kandaki. Especially this Prahotep and the dragon. I have to tell you, the situation is not good. Right outside my gates Shabako has seven times as many men as I do and garrisons in most of the other cities of Nubia. Now, I think we can hold out against a siege for a few months, and I hope that once it's known you're still alive, more of the country will rally to support you. But it will be a delicate business, and these Egyptians won't help. I don't think they should be allowed to wander about Nubia at will. It may be that they've killed the dragon of Derr just to set another monster in its place."

"Hathor isn't a monster!" Kandaki protested angrily. A string of beads fell out of her hair and rattled across the floor.

"Hold *still*, Kandaki!" ordered Amana. "I'm almost finished, but I'll never get it done if you keep squirming about like this. Now, I just need one or two more beads . . ."

Kandaki handed her the blue bead that Shabako's soldier had given her. "What's this?" asked Amana, looking at it doubtfully.

"One of Shabako's men gave it to me," replied Kandaki, "in return for a bunch of grapes. I think it will bring me luck."

Amana smiled and strung the bead in with the others. Kandaki tossed her head, and her hair rattled and bounced against her shoulders, just as it always had. "Hathor isn't a monster," she told Mandulis again. "If you'd seen her and spoken to her, you'd know that."

"Perhaps," he said. "But I haven't, and your friend Prahotep seems unusually eager that I shouldn't since he's willing to throw away any reward you might give him rather than take the creature into the city. Who knows what he's playing at? I think we should make sure that *everyone* on that boat is safely in my city tonight even if we have to bring them in in chains."

"They're my friends!" Kandaki said angrily. "And they saved my life. You will *not* use any violence against them or—or I'll—I'll appoint someone else as governor of Napata!"

"Kandaki!" cried Amana, shocked. "Is that any way to speak to Mandu?"

"I'm sorry, Uncle," Kandaki said. "I know you're the best man in Nubia, and the most loyal, and I owe you everything. But how can I agree to put chains on those who have helped me so much? What sort of queen would I be if I started my reign by imprisoning my friends?"

Mandu sighed. "The girl is right," he told his wife. "She can't, in honor, do anything but stand up for her friends. Very well, but try to persuade this Egyptian and his dragon to come in of their own free will. I don't like the thought of them at large in the country at all."

"Yes, Uncle," she said, "I was going to try that, anyway."

"Now," said Mandulis, "we'd better get along to the temple. Even my own troops won't believe you're alive unless they can see you with their own eyes."

When they came back into the courtyard of the palace, they found a huge crowd waiting. There were Mandu's guardsmen, with their long bows, gold-ringed spears, and red and white shields, and his servants carrying ostrich feather fans and red banners on posts of ivory; there were priests with shaven heads beating drums and priestesses shaking the high-pitched rattling sistrum and dancing.

Mandu showed Kandaki to a sedan chair—a kind of armchair on a stretcher—and four of his men picked up the posts and carried her, at shoulder height, out into the city. The people of Napata cheered madly and threw flowers at her. "Long live Queen Kandaki!" they yelled, loud enough to deafen her.

They proceeded slowly through the narrow streets of Napata to the temple of Amun and Apedemek, where the sedan chair was put down again, and Kandaki walked through the immense gateway with the cheering crowd behind her, to offer thanks to the gods for her safety.

She was standing before the altar in the middle of the ceremony of thanksgiving when she noticed one of Mandulis's soldiers pushing his way through the crowd to the governor of the city. The man reached his master and whispered in his ear. Mandulis, in turn, slid up to Kandaki and the priests of Amun and Apedemek. "Finish it quickly," he whispered. "Shabako is drawing up his troops, and I think he's going to attack."

The priest of Apedemek cut the ceremony short at once and ordered one of the musicians to sound his trumpet. In the silence that followed the trumpet blast, they all heard, faint but clear, the terrible shout of the war cry as the enemy advanced upon the city.

The soldiers turned and began to run out of the temple, heading for the walls to defend them. Mandulis drew his sword. He shoved Kandaki back toward the altar. "Wait here, my queen," he said grimly. "They won't get in." And already shouting orders, he followed his men.

Kandaki sat down heavily on the steps of the altar. Just for a minute she wished she'd taken Baki's advice and hidden somewhere for a few months instead of coming to Napata. The war had started, and she didn't feel ready for it at all. People were fighting for her now, maybe dying, and all she could do was sit. She felt hot and sick and frightened, and she wanted to cry.

"Don't be frightened, Queen," said the priest of Amun. "Lord Mandulis will hold the city for you."

"I'm not frightened," she said proudly. Her parents had always told her that kings and queens must never show fear, whatever they felt, or their followers would be afraid, too. "Is there anywhere in the temple where I can see what's going on?"

The two priests showed her out to the huge temple gateway, and they climbed up inside it to the top of the arch. From there they could see the whole city—the narrow streets of mud-brick buildings, the taller palace with its gardens, and the walls. Men were fighting on the walls; she could see Shabako's troops flinging ropes over the battlements and scrambling up, and Mandulis's men trying to throw them off. Arrows flew so thickly they looked like clouds of flies over the river. Swords flashed, and there were screams and bellows of rage. Dust billowed, and something somewhere was burning, releasing clouds of biting black smoke.

Some of Shabako's men had climbed the wall and were jumping down into the streets. The priest of Amun pulled at Kandaki's arm. "We should go into the temple, my lady," he said, "and lock the gate. Even if Lord Mandulis manages to drive them off, if one of them succeeds in finding and killing you, we'll have lost the war."

Reluctantly Kandaki climbed down from the gateway and allowed the priests to lock and bolt the immense doorway. They walked slowly back into the temple. They were in the first courtyard when they heard a shout of pleasure from in front of them, where the altar was. Kandaki stopped—and saw Kashta and twenty of his men running toward her.

"So it is you, Princess!" yelled Kashta, waving his spear. "Since the dragon didn't finish you, I will!"

The priest of Amun wailed and fell to the ground, covering his eyes. Kandaki spun on her heels and ran. She dodged around the columns of the courtyard and leaped over a flower bed. Kashta was right behind her. She grabbed a handful of stones and dried mud from the flower bed and flung it in his face. Kashta swore and kept on coming, blindly. She dodged and ran back through the columns. He crashed into one, dropped his spear, and staggered, his nose streaming blood. Kandaki ran into one of the temple storerooms, looking for a weapon, and found only jars of oil and a dead end. She turned; one of Kashta's men was in the doorway behind her. Quickly she pushed over a jar. It rolled into him, spilling oil, and he crashed to the ground backward. She jumped on top of him and tore his sword out of his hand.

The man behind him stabbed at her with his spear; she deflected it the way Baki had showed her and slashed at him. To her surprise and horror, the sword hit him, and he screamed, clutching a half-severed hand. Kandaki backed away, then turned and ran again. She came to a ladder and scrambled up it, panting, and raced along a roof. They were still after her. She jumped onto another roof and ran, then stopped. She'd reached the second courtyard, and before her there was only a sheer two-story drop to the hard pavement below. Behind her Kashta was advancing again, his spear at the ready. Kandaki braced herself, holding the sword in both hands. Thank the gods, she thought, they haven't got bows.

"How did you know I was here?" she asked Kashta, hoping to win time for someone to come and help. "How did you get into the temple?"

He sneered. "The whole city has been screaming aloud that you were going to the temple of Amun. Our main attack was just a diversion, to draw off old Mandulis and his troops. King Shabako showed me the entrance to a secret passageway into the temple and told me to find you and make sure you were properly dead this time."

"King Shabako!" she said. "Even if you kill me, he won't be a real king! Perhaps the pharaoh of Egypt will let him call himself a viceroy!"

Kashta paused. "He's a real king," he declared. "I had doubts—but not anymore. He has the Hand of Userr, the amulet given to the king of Nubia by the god Apedemek. Only a true king can hold it. That Egyptian was lying when he said Shabako had been negotiating with Pharaoh. Maybe Mandulis sent him."

"He didn't!" said Kandaki, but Kashta wasn't listening anymore. He was moving toward her again, grinning. Kandaki took a deep breath and clutched the sword. Maybe, she thought, maybe I can kill just one of them before they get me.

Then there was a sudden scream. Kashta spun around, and Kandaki looked up—and saw Baki pulling his sword out of one of Kashta's men. As she watched, he kicked sideways, tripping another, and knocked a third over the head, stunning him. He slipped past a fourth, dodged a fifth, and slid to a stop beside Kandaki.

"Coward!" he shouted at Kashta. "Twenty of you to fight one girl! If you've got any spirit, Kashta, come and fight me!"

"I've seen you before, Egyptian," said Kashta. "Where's your friend the liar?" He lunged at Baki.

Baki stepped sideways and caught the spear as it went by. He gave it a jerk, pulled it out of Kashta's hands, and tossed it hard into another of Kashta's men, killing him. Kashta's eyes widened. He drew his sword.

Baki grinned. "That's more like it," he said, and slashed at Kashta with his own blade.

Kandaki edged away, trying to leave Baki plenty of space. Kashta's soldiers jumped at her, and she had her hands full trying to ward them off. After she'd parried two or three thrusts, the men were wary, surprised to find that she could fence at all, and she crouched, facing them, her back to the drop. They lunged quickly and retreated. Kandaki's wrists ached from gripping the sword, and the hilt was slippery with sweat. She wondered how long she could keep parrying the thrusts, how soon it would be before one of them slipped through her guard. To her left, she could hear the clash and stamp and grunt of Kashta and Baki fighting furiously, but she didn't dare look away from the glaring eyes of her opponents.

Then there was a horrible grunt, and the soldiers in front of her fell back. She looked over just in time to see Kashta falling to the ground, blood spurting from his neck in great gouts. Baki pushed him aside with his foot and raised his sword again.

"That foreigner has killed Lord Kashta!" shouted one of the soldiers in horror.

"Then let's revenge him!" shouted another. And the soldiers closed in again.

But as Baki and Kandaki braced themselves to meet them, black smoke rose from the courtyard below, surrounding them in choking clouds.

"The temple's on fire!" one of the soldiers exclaimed.

"They fired the town earlier," said another. "It must have got into the temple granary."

"But we're on top of the stores," said a third. "We'll be burned alive!"

Nobody else said anything in answer; they were already running. Back across the roofs they went. At the top of the ladder one of the soldiers waved the smoke aside and shouted to Baki and Kandaki, "We'll leave you here to burn!" And then they were gone.

Coughing and choking in the smoke, Baki and Kandaki stumbled after them. But the ladder was lying on the pavement of the first courtyard, far below.

"Maybe there's another way down," said Kandaki.

They ran along the edge of the roof, back to the second courtyard. But there were no stairs, no ladders, and no way down. The smoke smelled oily, and Kandaki imagined the stores in the building under their feet, oil and grain, blazing hot enough to melt glass.

They reached Kashta's body and looked down into the second courtyard again—and saw a man standing in the yard below, looking up. For a moment Kandaki thought he was an unknown Nubian, and then she realized it was Prahotep, covered from head to foot in soot. "Baki!" he called to them. "Kandaki! Are you all right?"

"Yes," said Baki urgently. "But the temple's on fire. There's a ladder in the first courtyard. Will you let us down?"

"I'll let you down," Prahotep said. "But the temple's not on fire. I just made a bonfire in the arch under the gate, to scare off those soldiers. It's going out now. If you go back to the first courtyard, I'll move the ladder for you."

After she'd slid down the ladder, Kandaki ran to Prahotep and hugged him. "You shouldn't do that, Princess," he told her. "You've got soot on your dress."

"You've got soot all over you," she replied. "However did you get so black?"

He grinned. "Standing over the fire and fanning smoke. I threw all sorts of things on to make it really black. I'm glad it worked."

There was a hollow crack in the air above them, and Hathor dropped into the courtyard, her wings curved to brake her steep fall. She settled beside Prahotep and eyed him doubtfully. "Are you pretending to be a Nubian?" she asked.

"It's just soot," he replied, trying, without much success, to wipe it off his face. "What's happening in the city?"

"Shabako's men are retreating, and their main camp's on fire."

"Their camp's on fire?" asked Kandaki. "How did that happen?"

Hathor hissed. "When we saw the smoke coming from Napata, we thought it would be fairer if there was smoke coming from Shabako's camp as well. So I made a fire, and Prahotep dropped torches on them."

"That was after I'd begged Hathor to drop me off in the city, so I could help you before it was too late," said Baki.

"And Hathor and I were coming back with more torches," said Prahotep, "when we saw you and Baki fighting off twenty men at once. So we stopped, and I used the torches to build a bonfire instead. Hathor was waiting up above. If the fire didn't work, she was going to come down and help you."

"Oh, Hathor!" Kandaki said. "I'm sorry. I know you didn't want to get involved in human wars."

The dragon hissed softly, then licked her cheek. "I was a fool," she said. "I should have realized I was involved already. When we saw the city burning, we all knew we had to help you. Those beads in your hair are really very pretty. They look quite a lot like scales."

There was a shout of terror from the gate, and they turned to see another group of armed men pouring into the temple toward them. Archers fanned out beside the entrance, drawing their bows. Prahotep jumped in front of Hathor and spread his arms to shield her; Baki tried to elbow Kandaki behind him.

"Don't shoot!" someone shouted. "You might hit the queen!"

And Kandaki realized suddenly that these soldiers carried the red and white shields of Mandulis's troops. She pushed Baki aside. "Yes, don't shoot!" she shouted back at the archers. "These are my friends, and they have just saved my life—again!"

The archers lowered their bows. Just at that minute Mandulis ran through the gateway, followed by the priest of Apedemek, who must have run to fetch him when Kashta attacked. His eyes swept the scene in the courtyard, and he stopped. Then he walked on toward them slowly.

"Uncle Mandu," said Kandaki, before Mandulis could say anything, "Kashta came into the temple with twenty men, looking for me. Baki killed him, and Prahotep tricked the rest into thinking the temple was on fire so that they ran. Hathor and Prahotep set fire to Shabako's camp, forcing him to retreat. Do you still think they're dangerous?"

"Indeed, I do," replied Mandulis. He stopped in front of Kandaki, looking at them all: Baki, his hand on his sword, his chest and arms splashed with blood; Prahotep, covered in soot, still standing in front of Hathor and looking back warily; and the dragon, big as a horse and longer than an oxcart, her immense talons curled and gleaming. "Very dangerous," he said. "But to our enemies, Kandaki, to our enemies."

And he smiled at them all. "Welcome to Napata!"

7

The Sand Dragon

THE MORNING AFTER THE BATTLE MAN-
DULIS CALLED A COUNCIL OF WAR IN THE
great hall of his palace. He seated Kandaki on a throne at
the head of a long table of polished ebony, arranged his
officers along the sides, and took his own place at the foot.
Baki, Prahotep, and Hathor were admitted to the council
but didn't sit at the table since they were foreigners. The
two men were given stools to one side, and Hathor curled
up nervously between them, her tongue flickering. She
did not like being surrounded by so many humans at
once, and to judge by the looks some of the officers gave
her, they didn't like facing even one dragon.

Shabako's troops had managed to get the fire in their
camp under control quickly, and they had tightened the
ring around Napata. The city was now under siege.
Mandulis, in turn, had posted a heavy guard on the
walls.

"And I should never have relaxed the guard yesterday," he said. "If the walls had been fully manned, Shabako's men could never have got anywhere near them.
But I thought the men needed to see their queen."

"It's not your fault, Uncle," said Kandaki. "And even as it was, Shabako's men didn't get far into Napata. Except Kashta, and he used the tunnel, which we didn't know about."

"The priest of Amun knew about it!" said Mandulis grimly. "It was his private escape route if the city fell. And he's escaped by it now, and taken some of the temple treasure with him, the miserable coward. I've had the entrance blocked and posted a guard on it."

"How did Shabako know it was there?" asked Kandaki.

Mandulis sighed. "They're saying now in the enemy camp that Shabako has found the Hand of Userr."

"Kashta said something about that yesterday. I think I've heard of it before. Isn't it supposed to be a jewel that the lion god, Apedemek, gave my ancestor Userr, to protect him against his enemies?"

Mandulis nodded. "And it saved him in many battles, until he went into the marshes of Derr to fight the water dragon. But he never returned from Derr, and the charm was lost. Now Shabako claims to have found it. Whether he really has, I very much doubt; he has every reason to forge it. They say that only a true king of Nubia can use it, so if he can use it, it strengthens his lying claim to royalty. But he'd need a powerful magician to forge it, for it's supposed to have two properties. The first is the property of vision; it allows its owner to see things that are hidden. The second is the property of striking; an arrow fired from a bow drawn with the Hand of Userr cannot miss its target. The Hand's supposed to be shaped like an archer's wrist guard, and set with a jewel in the shape of an eye."

"Like the thing Prahotep . . ." Kandaki began, then stopped.

"Like what thing Prahotep?" asked Mandulis.

Kandaki didn't answer. She turned to Prahotep. He was sitting on his stool with an intent expression on his face, trying to follow the Nubian speech of the council. "Prahotep," Kandaki said, in Egyptian, "where's that thing you found in the marshes?"

"On the *Lucky Lady*," he replied. "I couldn't quite follow what you were saying. Is it important?"

"It might be. Hathor, please—none of us can get out of the city. Do you think you could go fetch it?"

The dragon uncurled. "If you like."

"I'll come with you," Prahotep said, getting to his feet.

"Please don't," Kandaki said quickly. "Hathor will be all right on her own. You know she will. And I'd like you here, to advise us."

Prahotep looked embarrassed. He sat down again. Hathor gave Kandaki a sideways look, her golden eyes gleaming. "Borrowing my favorite human," she remarked. "Sensible woman! I'll be back soon." And she padded out.

One of Mandu's officers, a tall young man named Aspelta, a northerner, gave Prahotep a look of intense dislike. "Shabako had a powerful magician to forge the Hand for him," he said, "The man Kashta met on the river, Nefersenet of Thebes—"

"Kashta didn't meet Nefersenet," Mandulis said patiently. "That was simply a story our friend Prahotep told him, to repay Shabako for his own lies."

"But I'd heard before that Shabako had dealings

with this Nefersenet!" Aspelta protested. "Last year a barge belonging to Shabako put in at my home city of Kawa, in the north, to buy oxen to help it round the rapids in the Belly of Stones. The captain said the cargo was a thanks offering to the god Horus, in Thebes, and when I heard Kashta's story, I checked, and discovered that the chief priest of Horus in Thebes is one Nefersenet, a notorious magician. What's more, I heard from a friend in Kawa only yesterday that this same Nefersenet set out for Nubia only a few weeks ago. I, for one, find it very suspicious that this foreigner, who commands a dragon like a great magician and destroyed the water dragon of Derr—which must have been done by magic, since all who've tried to do it by strength have failed—chose to tell Kashta that his name was Nefersenet. I think you were telling the truth then, Egyptian, but are lying now! Didn't Shabako pay you enough for forging the Hand?" He had spoken in Egyptian, to make sure Prahotep could understand him.

Baki jumped to his feet, his hand on his sword. "Are you out of your mind, Nubian?" he asked. "Nefersenet's dead!"

"Dead?" said Aspelta. "I've heard nothing about that, and I don't believe it!"

"It only happened a little while ago," Prahotep said quietly. "But, my lord Aspelta, Nefersenet was an important man. He would never have set out for Nubia in a sailing barge; he had a twenty-oared temple galley, with slaves to row it for him. I'm a nobody, the son of a poor fisherman. Nefersenet would have been very insulted to

hear that you'd mistaken me for him. As for command-
ing the dragon, you can see for yourself that I don't. It's
more like she commands me. From what you say, I
think Nefersenet may have forged a magic charm for
Shabako. He didn't set out for Nubia because of that,
though. He wanted a dragon for a magic spell, and he
followed us from Thebes. But as Baki said, he's dead
now, and if you don't believe me, you can send a boat
downriver to the Belly of Stones. His body will still be
lying there. Baki and I left him under the figurehead of
his ship, since his own men were in too much of a hurry
to bury it."

"So whether this Hand is real or not," said Mandulis,
quickly changing the subject, "it may allow Shabako to
see things that are hidden?"

"I'm sure it will," said Prahotep. "Nefersenet was a
very powerful magician."

Mandulis sighed. "It will be a great help to Shabako
that he has this thing, however he got it! There will be
plenty of people who'll say that since he has it, the god
Apedemek must have chosen him as king. And though
many of the lords of Nubia will stay loyal, as it happens,
many of the most loyal of them are still Shabako's prisoners in Meroë, and their families and supporters won't
help us, for fear that they'll be murdered if they do. Shabako's army outnumbers us seven to one. We're secure
in the city now, if we keep a strong watch on the walls,
but we can't expect to defeat the enemy in open battle.
I thought we could wait here for the rest of Nubia to
rally to us, but Shabako's men set fire to one of the city

granaries yesterday. We don't have enough supplies left now to last us more than a month. My friends, our case is desperate, unless we can get some help."

"Can't we send a small force of men to Meroë?" asked Kandaki. "If Shabako's men are all here, besieging us, he must have left the capital lightly guarded. Even a hundred men should be able to take it. And when they took it, they could release the prisoners and free our supporters to act according to their loyalty."

"How can we send a force to Meroë?" Mandulis asked wearily. "Shabako's troops are concentrated along the river, and he has garrisons in all the major cities; we could never get a hundred men through, even at night. And if they could get through, there are three sets of rapids between here and Meroë; they couldn't travel quickly, and Shabako's troops would come on them and destroy them."

Prahotep had been listening with the blank expression on his face. "Excuse me," he said now, "but doesn't the river bend northward for a couple of hundred miles from Napata, and then turn south again? If you sent a troop of men overland directly west, they'd avoid most of Shabako's men, cut across the bend, and strike the river just above Meroë after only a few days."

"Well, yes," said Mandulis, "but they'd die of thirst before they reached it. The land route to Meroë is over a barren desert, and we couldn't possibly smuggle donkeys out of the city to carry enough water for the journey. There are water holes in it, here and there; but their locations change, and only the beasts of the desert know where they are now."

"You've forgotten Hathor," said Prahotep, his eyes beginning to gleam. "She could find them. And she could watch the enemy camp from the sky as well and find a way for a hundred men to slip out of Napata at night. With luck Shabako wouldn't even know they'd gone. And when they reached Meroë, they could take it in the queen's name."

"By Amun and Apedemek!" exclaimed Mandulis, slapping the table. "I believe you're right!"

Aspelta leaped to his feet. "I volunteer to lead the force to Meroë!" he shouted.

"No!" said Kandaki, standing up. "I will lead it myself!"

"It will be a hard and dangerous journey, my queen," said Mandulis reprovingly. "You must stay here and keep up the courage of your troops."

"But I have troops in Meroë and the south that need their courage kept up even more!" Kandaki protested. "They still believe I'm dead, and will probably go on believing it, unless they see me. And, Uncle, you know yourself that I'm not safe here either. If we lose, I'd rather die in Meroë, sitting on my father's throne, than here, borrowing your judgment chair."

Mandulis sighed. "Very well, and you have a point. You need to be present in Meroë to convince the rest of the country you're alive. But you cannot lead the troops yourself. I would escort you myself, but I can't abandon my city while it's under seige, and the enemy would soon discover it if I did. As the commander in chief of your army I am giving Aspelta charge of the expedition,

and his chief responsibility will be to ensure your safety.
I will let him pick a hundred men. And Prahotep will
have to go, too, with the dragon."

"If the Egyptian doesn't command the dragon," said
Aspelta, glaring at Prahotep, "why does he have to
come? I don't like Egyptians. We know them in Kawa;
they've sacked our city many times."

"And you deserved it, too, from the sound of you,"
said Baki, glaring back at Aspelta. "Prahotep and I *both*
will come, unless the queen commands us to stay. But
where is Hathor? She should be back by now."

There was a moment of silence and then a rush at
the door, and Hathor herself burst in. Her eyes were
blazing, her chest and forelegs were covered in blood,
and she looked so terrifying that some of the officers
jumped under the table. She was carrying a lion skin in
her mouth.

"Hathor!" cried Prahotep, running over to her.
"You're hurt!"

Hathor dropped the lion skin. "That foul, stinking,
murdering *thief* Shabako has stolen *my treasure*!" she
said, and gave a long, hissing shriek. She fanned her
wings so hard the table jumped. "I came to the *Lucky
Lady* and found his filthy men looting it! My treasure!
All my lovely things!" She struck the lion skin with her
claws, knocking it the length of the room; it unrolled,
and the golden wrist guard flew out of it and clattered
against a column. "I stooped on them; I struck them; I
threw them out of the boat. I filled the reeds with blood!
But then more came running, with archers and spear-

men, the dirty cowards! I grabbed the jewel you wanted and flew. They have the rest, the revolting brutes—all my hoard, everything my mother left me, and her mother before her! All gone!"

"Hathor!" Prahotep said, clinging to her foreleg. "You're hurt, you're bleeding, please, be still, let me see...."

The dragon flopped down, hissing like a fire in a marsh. "It's only a scratch," she told him contemptuously. "I can heal that. But not the loss of my treasure."

"When we have defeated Shabako," Kandaki declared, "you shall have your treasure back, every piece of it, and if there's anything that's been lost or destroyed, I will replace it from the royal treasury of Nubia and add as much again, to compensate you for your loss."

"Oh, that is royal!" said Hathor, picking up her head again. "That is a decent, queenly thing to do, Princess! What can we do to defeat that disgusting villain? I'll teach the brute to steal from *me*!"

"We're going to try to cross the desert to Meroë," Prahotep told her soothingly, "and we do need your help. Please lie still! Someone fetch a doctor!"

"I don't need any stupid human doctors rubbing foul ointments into me," Hathor returned. "I can do better than that myself." She began licking her chest, curving her long green neck double. Her wings jerked several times with outrage but eventually relaxed.

Mandulis picked up the gold wrist guard and examined it; unlike most noblemen, he could read. "'Foremost in Nubia,'" he read slowly, "'Lion, beloved of Apedemek, see with the god's eye, and strike without error! So should a king rule wisely, seeing truth and sparing the innocent.'" He looked up at Kandaki, his eyes shining. "It *is* the Hand of Userr. This is what the old books say was written on it. Where did you find it?"

"Prahotep found it," replied Kandaki, "in the marshes of Derr after we killed the water monster. We didn't know what it was."

Mandulis pressed it into her hand. "It is the greatest treasure of your house," he said, "and Apedemek himself must have brought it to you, to stop the lies of the usurper Shabako and show all Nubia that you are the true queen." Then he picked up the lion skin that had been wrapped around the jewel. "And this must be your father's cloak, the king's cloak from Meroë. I wanted to give you a lion skin cloak yesterday, but I had none. I'm glad you brought it."

"That's Prahotep's," Hathor said, looking up sharply. "I gave it to him. And the bracelet ought to be his, too. He found it."

"But I can't keep either, not here in Nubia," said Prahotep. "They're far too grand for me." He went over to Mandulis, took the cloak, draped it around Kandaki's shoulders, and pinned it. Then he took a step back, knelt, and raised his hands in the Egyptian way. "Long life and prosperity to you, Queen of Nubia!"

"Long live Queen Kandaki!" shouted all the Nubian officers, jumping to their feet.

"But how do I use the Hand?" asked Kandaki, holding the golden charm before her. The blue jewel of the eye, gold-rimmed, stared back at her.

"I don't know," said Mandulis. "I don't think anyone does. It's something you'll have to discover. If we're to send this force to Meroë, we'd better get to work equipping it right away. It would be best if you left tonight."

They set off that night before moonrise. When Hathor had finished cleaning her wound, she flew over the whole of Napata at a great height and, on returning, reported that the enemy had only a very light guard to the south of the city and that there was a steep gully that led from the Nile Valley into the desert and could give them cover. So the hundred men slipped down a rope hung in an angle of a guard tower in the dark and waited for their leaders to join them.

Mandulis hugged Kandaki roughly. "Good-bye, my queen," he whispered. "I know you have a lion's spirit, like your father, but remember that all the country depends upon you and be careful! And you, Aspelta—you look after her."

"I will die myself before I let any harm come to my sovereign lady!" the young officer declared proudly.

"Good! Spoken like a loyal Nubian. As for you"—Mandulis turned to Hathor and the two Egyptians—"you've saved her for us twice in the past. Look after her now, too. Good-bye!"

The humans slid down the rope; Kandaki was just aware of Hathor gliding off the wall, vanishing into the darkness above, where she would keep watch for them. At the foot of the wall the party began walking quickly through the chill black winter night.

They slipped past Shabako's men in the darkness,

found the gully Hathor had described, and began climbing. The way became rocky and uneven as they left the valley, and the air became colder, thin, smelling of stone. The moon rose as they emerged from the gully onto the high desert, showing a vast, empty plain of rock, broken only by a few thistles and scrubby thorns. They paused to catch their breaths and eat a few bites from their packs, then began walking westward, following the moon as it moved across the sky.

The sun rose behind them, huge and red, and the rock of the desert turned the color of dried blood. Hathor glided down out of the fading dark, her shadow trailing like a patch of ink behind her. "You should go to the north a little," she told them. "There's a water hole in a valley there, about three miles away. I'll fly in that direction, and if you start to go wrong, I'll tell you."

By the time they reached the water hole, it was getting hot. Kandaki's legs ached, and she had a stitch in her side. The lion skin cloak, which she'd been glad of during the night, was horribly hot, heavy, and scratchy now. But she didn't complain. All the men were carrying heavy packs of supplies, and they'd refused to let her carry one as well. They, she thought, must feel even worse than she did. The muddy water, a shallow puddle left by some trickle of brief rain, tasted delicious.

They rested at the water hole during the hottest part of the day and set out again in the evening. Hathor found another water hole for them the next morning, this one to the south, and they stopped there again.

Kandaki hadn't liked Aspelta because he had accused

Prahotep, but she had to admit that he was an excellent officer. He always saw that everything was done fairly, and he looked after his men, encouraging them when they were tired and cheering them up when they were discouraged. He said nothing whatever to the two Egyptians, but he didn't make any trouble for them, either. Now he came up to Kandaki again and saluted. "We've made good time, my queen!" he told her. "One of my men, who's hunted in this desert, reckons we've covered fifty miles in the past two days. At this rate we should hit the Nile again in only another three days."

Hathor, who was sitting nearby, hissed. She had not caught any game that night, didn't like the dried meat and salt fish that the humans offered her, and she was irritable. "Tomorrow will be harder," she told Aspelta. "There's sand ahead. I don't reckon on finding anything to eat tomorrow, and I should think that with those ridiculous little feet of yours, you won't make very good time."

Aspelta looked momentarily disheartened. Sand would be much harder to march over.

"There are supposed to be sand dragons in the middle of that bit of desert," Kandaki said, to cheer the dragon up.

Hathor hesitated, one forefoot in the air. "Dragons in a sand desert?" she said doubtfully. "It's not a good place, with the hunting so bad. Of course, perhaps it was better in the past. My mother always said that when she was young, the whole of the Nubian desert was grassland, and her mother used to catch elephants there, and zebra. Now, of course, there are only a few lizards, which isn't enough for anyone to live on. But perhaps these dragons hunt the fringes of the sand." She was beginning to look excited. "I'm going hunting now. I'll look for them." She bounded off, flapped heavily, then glided aloft.

Hathor did not find any sand dragons that day, but she did find a gazelle, which pleased her. Aspelta had the half of the animal she hadn't eaten on the spot butchered and gave it to five of his men to carry. "Now you won't have to go hungry tomorrow," he told her. That pleased her, too.

The next march was awful. The sand was soft, and it slipped underfoot. After ten minutes their legs ached, and after an hour they were shaking and numb. What was worse, when day dawned, Hathor could find no water hole. The sand became so hot they couldn't bear to touch it and wrapped blankets around their feet. They tried to rest at noon, but between the blazing sun and the burning sand, they couldn't and had to stumble on. Late in the afternoon Hathor glided down and told them she had found a water hole, but it was sixteen miles off—seven or eight hours' walk, at the speed they were managing. Still, they rested in the evening and at midnight drank the last of the water they'd taken from the previous hole and set out.

"The water is in a rocky cleft in the sand," Hathor had told them. "The sand piles up on either side, so you'll need to climb to get to it. Just before you come to it, there are a few big pits. Go past those to the right, then double back into the valley."

It was late in the morning when they reached the

pits, and they all were half blind with exhaustion and thirst. But tired as they were, the men gave a yell of pleasure at seeing the landmark and began running. As one of them ran along the very edge of a pit, the loose sand slipped under his feet, and he slid down to the bottom. He was climbing to his feet again, swearing, when the sand under his feet heaved. He turned—and screamed. The sand moved again; there was a crunch, another scream, and then silence.

The men in front stopped and turned back at the screams, and the rest of the party hurried forward. When they came to the edge of the pit, they gasped or wailed in horror. Crouched at the bottom was a sand-colored monstrosity the size of an ox. It was shaped something like a crab, short and squat and many-legged; but the blunt yellow-brown head was eyeless, and two small scythelike arms waved, slashing the flesh off the body of the man who'd fallen and shoving it into the wet red mouth. Two larger arms ended in massive, razor-edged claws, and the stiff, jointed legs were fringed with dull gray hairs.

Aspelta gave a shout of rage when he saw the thing eating one of his soldiers. He tossed his pack aside and pulled his bow out of the strap that secured it. Quickly he strung it and shot at the monster.

The arrow slid uselessly off the thing's hard back. The monster jumped and spun toward Aspelta, its huge claws waving.

"If you don't mind arrows," whispered Aspelta, "we'll see if you like something bigger!" He picked up his spear and charged into the pit.

He slid down to the bottom and thrust, furiously, at the joint in one claw. The thing made a shrill clicking sound. Its claw jerked—and the spear broke. Quickly Aspelta dropped and rolled under the claw, drawing his sword. He got to his knees and chopped at the thing's belly. The sword rang, flashing sparks, rang again. The monster's armor was undented. It slid backward, and its scythe arms flashed. Aspelta gave a gasp of pain. He thrust with his sword again, directly toward the mouth this time—and the sword turned against a scythe and snapped. Desperate now, Aspelta again rolled underneath the massive shell and began climbing the pit wall behind the thing. The monster stood for a moment, clicking, then turned around. It lowered its eyeless shell and stood still, its legs splayed. Aspelta, panting, scrambled harder; the sand slid under his feet. The crab scuttled toward him.

"No!" shouted Kandaki in horror, looking wildly around.

"No!" shouted Prahotep, behind her. "Aspelta, *lie still!*" He grabbed handfuls of sand and began throwing it against the side of the pit opposite the young officer. The crab thing paused, clicking, jerking its scythe arms up and down. "Lie still!" Prahotep shouted to Aspelta again, "It can't see you; it only feels where you are from the movement of the sand!"

Aspelta lay still. His eyes were very white, and he was sweating. Blood was streaming from a gash on his sword arm. Prahotep threw a few more handfuls of sand. The crab thing turned toward him, rushed, stopped. It clicked fretfully and again stood still, as though it were listening.

When Prahotep tossed another handful of sand, it again rushed at it and again stopped, waiting.

"How do I get out?" called Aspelta. The sand shifted as he called, and the thing at once began to move toward him. This time Kandaki kicked some sand into the pit, and it stopped, confused.

Baki was unslinging his bow. "We'll all shoot it," he said. "If we can get the joints of its legs, we should be able to cripple it." He took careful aim and fired at a joint in one of the legs. All around the top of the pit, the soldiers did the same. In a moment the air was black with arrows. But in another moment the thing was standing, unharmed, in a pile of shafts.

Baki set his teeth. "Can somebody make it open its mouth? That isn't armored." Kandaki snatched a spear and began stabbing it into the side of the pit in front of her. The thing scuttled toward her. She stopped, and it picked itself up, dropping its scythe feet away from its wet mouth. Again there was a cloud of arrows, aimed at the only gap in its armor. But the scythe feet swept up, and the arrows were all pushed aside. The thing began to shrill. It felt its way back around the pit, moving toward Aspelta.

Baki drew his sword. "I'm coming in after you," he said.

"No!" gasped Aspelta. "It will kill you, too!"

"As Amun lives," exclaimed Baki, "I don't stand around and watch when companions are about to be eaten!" He turned to Prahotep. "You're the clever one," he said. "Think of something! Think of something or I go in after it!"

"I'm trying to!" groaned Prahotep. "I can't!"

Kandaki reached over and took Baki's bow. "What are you doing?" Baki demanded, angrily. "If *I* can't shoot it in the mouth, *you* won't be able to; you barely know how to draw that.''

''But I have the Hand of Userr,'' she answered, ''and we'll see if it will work for me.'' She slipped the golden bracelet around her wrist, set an arrow to the bowstring, drew the bow, and stood still a moment, looking down the shaft. ''Make it turn this way,'' she ordered. The others all hurled handfuls of sand on the wall of the pit in front of her, and the crab lifted itself and turned directly toward her. The shell that faced her was blank as a sand dune, blind, and merciless. The scythe arms waved before the red mouth. ''O Apedemek,'' Kandaki whispered, ''if you ever loved my house, let me strike without error now!'' Her fingers trembled as she released the arrow.

It flew straight and dark. The hooked arms swept before the mouth, but the arrow seemed to twist between them, down into the red mouth, and into the huge body within. The crab thing shrilled like a million cicadas. It jerked up and down, turning around and around. It slipped, fell to the bottom of its pit, lay on its back, its legs curling into its armored belly. Then it was still.

Aspelta scrambled toward the top of the pit. Baki ran around and offered him a hand to help him out. Aspelta looked into his face a moment, then took the offered hand and pulled himself up. ''Thank you,'' he said to Baki, ''and you''—turning to Prahotep. ''I accused you unjustly, but you saved my life.''

''The queen saved your life,'' replied Baki, slapping him on the back, ''but we'll take the credit if you like.''

8

Meroë

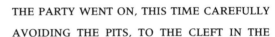

THE PARTY WENT ON, THIS TIME CAREFULLY AVOIDING THE PITS, TO THE CLEFT IN THE rock where they found the water hole—incredibly, not a mere hole, but a tiny green valley, full of trees in blossom, with a spring that gushed from the stone, ran a few hundred feet, and vanished into the sand. Hathor was waiting for them, curled up on a patch of grass.

"We found one of your sand dragons," said Aspelta, collapsing beside the water.

"Where?" asked Hathor, leaping to her feet. When they told her, she flew off to look at it, then, as quickly, flew back.

"You call that thing a dragon?" she demanded in disgust. "You humans are appallingly sloppy about names. First a big fish was a water dragon, and now a big land crab is a sand dragon! They're monsters, nothing like dragons at all! What would you think if I called baboons hairy humans and ostriches fast humans because you all had two legs? I only hope whoever named your other Nubian dragons was a bit more honest! . . . What's Aspelta done to his arm?"

"The sand dragon did it," said Aspelta.

"Sand *monster,*" corrected Hathor. "Let me see to it."

"Let her," urged Prahotep. "She can heal it very quickly."

Aspelta sat still and allowed Hathor to lick his cut clean. It was a deep gash, and though the bleeding stopped under Hathor's quick tongue, it was plain that Aspelta wouldn't have the full use of his sword arm for a while. "I'm sorry, Queen," he told Kandaki miserably. "Lord Mandulis told me to look after you, and you've ended up saving me! I attacked without thinking, and now I'll be a burden to the whole expedition. Let—let Prahotep take command in my place."

"Aspelta, you couldn't have acted more bravely," said Kandaki, "and Prahotep doesn't speak enough Nubian to command the men."

"And I can't use a sword, even with a whole sword arm," put in Prahotep. "I'm no soldier. No, you keep command. But maybe Baki can help you, until you're completely better again."

So Baki was made assistant commander of the expedition.

They rested in the green oasis until the moon rose, then set out again. After only a few miles they reached the end of the sand, and the march became easier. And the next night, in the gray before dawn, they came down out of the desert into the warmth of the Nile Valley. Meroë was now less than a day's journey ahead.

Kandaki remembered that Kashta had had a country house in the region, so the tired and hungry expedition marched on until they came to it and, when they came to it, marched in. They locked Kashta's servants in the cellars and helped themselves to food and drink, then washed and rested for the rest of the day. Any stranger who came to the door was told that the house steward's mother had died, and the household was in mourning and not receiving visitors, so they were perfectly secure. Kandaki had never realized that a bath and a bed could seem the very pinnacle of luxury.

In the evening they questioned some of the servants about the situation in Meroë. Many of them were quite eager to be helpful when they learned that Kashta was dead and couldn't come back to punish them. The royal city had been left under the command of Shabako's new wife, Abar, who was in charge of a garrison of about eighty men, most of whom were busy guarding Shabako's hostages. But it seemed that the enemy was nervous. A strict watch was being kept on all the gates, and the markets in the city were closed.

"That's awkward," Aspelta said. "We don't have enough men to storm the walls. And if we tried to besiege Meroë, Shabako would arrive with reinforcements before we could achieve anything."

"Worse than that," said Kandaki, "the enemy inside the city would almost certainly kill the hostages if we attacked openly. We'll have to find some way to get right into the royal palace before we start fighting. We need a clever scheme."

Everyone looked at Prahotep.

Prahotep winced. "I suppose we could sail in," he

said after a minute. "Kashta kept a boat here. I noticed it when we marched in; it's a sixteen-oared barge."

Everyone else looked blank. "Why would they let us in by water if they wouldn't let us in by land?" asked Kandaki.

"Because they'd recognize Kashta's boat," answered Prahotep. "Since Kashta's servants here hadn't heard that Kashta's dead, they probably haven't heard in Meroë either. If we arrived in Kashta's barge, pretending to be some of Kashta's men, come from Napata with a message for Abar . . ."

"We'd be admitted to the palace at once!" cried Aspelta. "Ushered into Lady Abar's presence—where we draw our swords and finish her and her forces on the spot!"

"Abar is my cousin!" Kandaki protested. "I know she was wicked to join Shabako; but she always was a vain, stupid, timid girl, and he flattered her and bullied her until she'd do anything he told her. I don't want her killed unless there's no other choice. We draw our swords and take her *prisoner*, Aspelta. But how many of us can fit in the barge, Prahotep? With sixteen oars it won't be big enough for all of us."

Prahotep grimaced. "It will take a few passengers, besides the oarsmen, but I think twenty-five, thirty people are the most it can carry. The rest of the party will have to get into Meroë by the gate."

"The party in the boat could attack the garrison on the walls and throw open the gates as soon as they're inside the city!" Aspelta said eagerly.

"Then the rest of the garrison, in the palace, will start executing prisoners," said Kandaki. "No. We'll have to trick them into letting us in. The party that comes in by boat will have to tell Abar—tell her—"

"—that Shabako wants some oxen to help build a siege wall around Napata!" finished Prahotep, starting to smile. "And they'll say that Kashta himself stopped at his country house and is rounding up ox drivers and carts in the countryside and that Abar is to send an official out to meet them and bring them into Meroë while he collects more oxen. Then the rest of our men disguise themselves as ox drivers, load the weapons in the carts under some straw, and wait for the official. He escorts them into the heart of Meroë, and they seize the palace."

Aspelta gave a whistle of admiration and looked at Baki, who'd been his firm friend since the sand dragon. Baki grinned. "Told you he was clever," he said proudly.

Prahotep shook his head. "It's not a very clever plan, really," he said. "There's too much that can go wrong. Can anyone else think up a better one?"

No one could, and it was decided that Aspelta should lead the party that entered the city by boat, with Prahotep to advise him and to steer the barge; an Egyptian wouldn't be too noticeable in the party if he kept his mouth shut. Kandaki and Baki would be with the ox-carts, and Hathor would spy out the territory around Meroë and find a good place for the others to wait. There were a dozen oxen at Kashta's farm, and five carts, and the ox-driving party loaded these at once. They would travel much more slowly than the group on the boat and so had to set out first.

Night was falling as Kandaki climbed onto the first

oxcart. She would have to hide under the straw with the weapons when it entered the city because people in Meroë might well recognize her. Prahotep and Aspelta came to the gate to say good-bye.

Looking at them, standing there in the dusk, Kandaki had a sudden cold feeling at the back of her neck and in the pit of her stomach. "What if it doesn't work?" she asked Prahotep. "What if they *have* heard in Meroë that Kashta's dead, or if somebody recognizes someone in your party, or if they've just had some other message from Shabako that makes them sure you're lying?"

"In that case, my queen," said Aspelta, "at least you'll be safely outside the gate. It will be up to you to find another way into the city."

"But *you*'ll be inside the palace, surrounded by the enemy!"

"Yes," said Prahotep. "Well, it was the best plan I could think of. I hope it does work. If anything happens to me, Kandaki . . . please, look after Hathor. It isn't her business to die in a human war."

"It isn't your war, either!" Kandaki exclaimed angrily. "You're not even Nubian!"

"Oh, I don't know," Prahotep answered. He gave her a rather lopsided smile. "In Egypt I never had any luck at anything. And I could never care for Pharaoh as I care for you. You'll be a wonderful queen, Kandaki, if you get the chance. If I can help you, I'm glad."

But he didn't look glad. He looked frightened and miserable, as though he couldn't wait to get the whole thing over. Kandaki remembered how he hated fighting.

"There are always risks in war," said Aspelta, "but I

think, Queen, that this plan of Prahotep's is the safest way we have of taking the city."

Aspelta, of course, had expected to be a warrior ever since he was a small boy; he was excited, not frightened. Kandaki sighed, leaned over, and hugged Aspelta, then kissed Prahotep. "Be careful!" she told them both, and the oxcart set off.

They rumbled and jolted southward for a few hours, and then Hathor stooped out of the moonlight and told them that the barge had set sail and that she had found a palm grove near the north gate of Meroë that would be a good place for their party to wait.

"I'll meet you there," she said. "I'm going to rest, and I'll check on the boat in the morning."

They arrived at the palm grove well before dawn, and settled down to rest—to sleep a little, if they could—before the dangerous day ahead.

The sun rose with a white shimmer in the east. Kandaki went to the south edge of the grove and looked out at the towering walls of Meroë. It seemed a lifetime since she'd left the city, tied and bundled into Kashta's boat. Now she was coming home. She wondered, with sick uncertainty, how many of the men she'd spoken to the previous evening would still be alive at this day's end.

Hathor flew out of the palms, soaring high out of sight. In a little while she returned and reported that Aspelta's party had sailed boldly up to the royal docks and, apparently, been welcomed and accepted. Now there was nothing to do but wait.

Wait they did. The morning dew faded into the air;

the sun climbed; the air grew hot. A few local villagers passed the palm grove, going to their fields or driving their flocks of goats. No one came from the city.

"Something's gone wrong," Kandaki said late in the morning.

"Give it a bit more time," Baki told her. "You know how clever Bad-luck is; his schemes always work."

"He's not a magician!" Kandaki said wretchedly. "He didn't have some charm to *make* people believe him; he had to rely on convincing them. And if they had heard that Kashta was dead . . . they'd kill them all!"

Hathor hissed. "I can fly Baki inside the gates," she said, "if you want to attack now."

Kandaki chewed her lip. "We'll wait until noon," she said reluctantly. "If no one's come by then, we'll have to try to find another way in."

Just at that minute there was a blast on a trumpet, and they ran to the edge of the grove to see two royal officials in white robes, holding ostrich feather fans, with a trumpeter and two soldiers, proceeding from the city directly toward them.

"It's worked!" Baki exclaimed happily. "Come on, Queen—into the cart!"

Hathor flapped up to hide in the palms, and Kandaki jumped into her oxcart and pulled the straw over herself. She heard the officials swish up to the Nubian soldier Aspelta had put in charge of the party. "You are Lord Kashta's ox drivers?" one asked sharply.

"That's right," said the soldier.

"Your friend Kenna wants you to bring your men

and carts into Meroë now. He tells you to hurry, the way you did at the oasis in the sands."

"We're coming . . ." began the soldier, but Baki suddenly pushed forward, drawing his sword.

"My *friend* Kenna?" he asked, in plain Egyptian. "As we did at the oasis? Kenna was an enemy of mine, and we met a hidden danger at the oasis! What have you done to our friends?"

The official didn't answer. Kandaki jumped out of the cart, throwing the straw aside. "Arrest them!" she ordered.

The officials looked at her, and their jaws dropped. "It's the princess Kandaki!" one exclaimed.

"It's the *queen* Kandaki," Kandaki corrected him, as her men closed around the officials and disarmed their men. "Answer my friend's question. What have you done to our friends?"

"We are the loyal servants of King Shabako," one of the men said, his face setting. "We'll tell you nothing."

"If you don't answer me," Kandaki said slowly, "I'll . . . give you to my dragon. Hathor!"

Hathor slid out of the trees and landed before the two men, curving her talons. Her golden eyes glowed with rage. "I heard everything. What have you done to Prahotep? Sspeak, you ssavagesss," she hissed, "or I'll tear you to shredsss!"

Both men looked absolutely sick with terror. One fell onto his face. "Mercy!" the other screamed. "Your friends are imprisoned in the palace, in the storerooms. We'd received a message from Shabako last night, saying that Kashta was dead and that a party of the enemy had escaped Napata by night and would try to enter Meroë. When your friends arrived, we knew they were lying; we overpowered them, and we questioned them about where the rest of you were. The Egyptian begged for mercy and told us where to find you. We have men inside the gate, ready to shoot you all down as you enter, but he tricked us, as you saw, and delivered a warning to you instead!''

"That's Bad-luck, all right," said Baki. "Where is he now? And Aspelta and the rest?"

"In the palace, as I said!" the official gabbled. "Twelve of your party were killed, but the rest are locked up, awaiting the king's orders. Please, my lady, please, don't let the monster eat me!"

"I don't eat rotten meat," said Hathor. "You filthy, treacherous ape!" She turned to Kandaki. "Do you want to attack the gate?"

"Not if there are archers posted there," Kandaki answered. She nodded to her men. "Tie these jackals up. We're going to have to think of another way into the city."

She went to the well in the middle of the date grove and sat down. Her heart was beating very hard, and her palms were wet. Shabako had realized that they'd left Napata; he must have sent a boat to Meroë at top speed. He must have used the fake Hand of Userr, as he had when he discovered the secret passageway into the temple in Napata.

Suppose there was a secret passageway into Meroë as

well? If the priests of Amun had one in one city, they might well have one in another. Suppose she could use the real Hand and find it? But how could she use it? True, it had worked when she killed the sand dragon, but then she'd used it like an ordinary wrist guard. How could she use it to see what was hidden? Would it work for a queen the way it would for a king? Would it work at all?

She had to try. The golden bracelet was still on her wrist. She turned it and stared into the blue eye. "Please," she whispered to the gods, "please, I must help my friends! Show me a way into Meroë!"

The blue eye stared back. Kandaki felt dizzy. For a moment she thought she would faint. But she kept her eyes fixed on the stone. She felt as though she were falling—but falling *upward,* into the sky and not away from it. Then the jewel seemed to fog over.

She could see, tiny at first but growing suddenly larger, the inner sanctuary of the temple of Amun in Meroë. She recognized the statue of the god, standing before a figure of his sacred ram at the high altar. She seemed to be rushing toward it. The ram figure—tall as a horse—swung aside, and she was swooping down a steep flight of stone steps and along a narrow corridor lined with great slabs of stone. She twisted, and the corridor burrowed through raw earth, swung around again, and rushed up another flight of steps. Then she was on a stone landing beside the river. She turned and saw Meroë behind her, the northern walls rising high. Before her was a tiny shrine of Amun, with its own small ram. The ram nodded its head and faded into a fog. She was staring into the blue eye of the Hand of Userr.

Kandaki drew a deep breath. She dried her palms on her skirt and went back to the others.

"We must go down to the river," she told them, "and look for a stone boat landing with a shrine of the god Amun. Bring your weapons."

"Where are we going?" asked Baki, but she didn't answer him, afraid that what she'd seen was nothing more than a fantasy born of her own fear and desperation.

They left the officials tied up in the palm grove and marched quickly down to the river. Kandaki hesitated there, trying to remember. The walls had loomed above her in the vision. She turned right, going toward the city.

They had not gone far when they reached it: a small stone landing with a shrine of Amun. There was a boat drawn up at it, and a man selling fish. He gave a shout of alarm when the group of seventy men, armed and grim, appeared on the landing, and a howl of terror when he saw Hathor. He shoved away from the bank, but Kandaki ignored him. She looked along the landing, trying to find the entrance to the passageway. There was no sign of it. She set her teeth angrily, and stared at the tiny figure of a ram. Then she caught her breath. Slowly she went to it and took the stone head in her fingers. She pulled it down.

There was a clunk, and one of the stone paving slabs dropped inward, revealing a flight of steps.

"As Amun lives," whispered Baki, looking at Kandaki in awe. "You used the Hand!"

Kandaki nodded, feeling weak. "This leads up to the

main altar in the temple of Amun,'' she said. ''The temple is just a block from the royal palace. When we come
out of the passageway, we can attack at once. They
won't expect us at the palace, and they must have most
of their guards waiting for us at the north gate. Come
on!'' She plunged into the passageway.

It was dark, as it had not been in the vision; after
the first few yards they stumbled along in total black-
ness. Kandaki went first, feeling her way, followed by
Baki and then Hathor; she could hear the rustle of the
dragon's wings in the darkness and the whisper of her
tail as it dragged along the earth. Then she tripped over
a paving slab; she had reached the first part of the tunnel, the part lined with stone. She groped on.

She stubbed her toe against the bottom step, hissed
a warning to the others, and began climbing. At the top
she nearly banged her head. She stood in the dark, fum-
bling against the rock above her, Baki pressing against
one shoulder and the dragon's smooth scales brushing
the other. There was a hollow in the rock and a catch.
She pulled it.

There was a creak and the sound of stone shifting,
and then light poured in. Kandaki leaped up the last
steps into the dimly lit sanctuary of the temple of Amun.
A fat, shaven-headed priest, who'd been cleaning the
floor, dropped his bucket and broom with a screech and
ran. Kandaki yelled and ran into the temple, and behind
her ran the others, shouting and cheering and, in Hathor's case, bounding and hissing. They tore through the
three courtyards and out the gate. Hathor jumped into

the air and glided upward, turning back and forth above them. In the city outside, people scattered out of their way, while others came running onto the roofs of their houses to see what was happening.

"It's the queen!" shouted someone, recognizing Kandaki. And suddenly everyone began to cheer. They swept up to the palace gates with a shouting crowd behind them. Hathor swooped down before them to the gate.

There were only four men guarding the entrance to the palace, and they turned and ran. Kandaki and the others poured through, into the house Kandaki remembered so well—the courtyard with its fountain, the antechamber with its red-painted columns. There were a dozen of the enemy at the entrance to the great throne room, and they put up a fight; but the fight didn't last more than a minute. Kandaki flung open the doors and, with Hathor behind her on one side and Baki, sword drawn, on the other, marched into her father's hall of judgment.

Her cousin Abar was sitting on her mother's throne, wearing her mother's best necklace, the gold one with the hawk pendant, and her hair strung with gold so that she looked like something made by a goldsmith. She was a little older than Kandaki, a small, plump, round woman, with a soft face and huge dark eyes that everyone always admired. Now the eyes were white-rimmed with terror. Abar shrank back against the chair when she saw Kandaki. Then she saw Hathor, screamed, and fainted. Kandaki marched up, dragged her cousin off the throne, and sat down in it herself.

"Long live Queen Kandaki!" roared her soldiers, and

behind them, the crowd, still pouring into the palace, took up the shout: "Long live Kandaki, daughter of Arkamon! Long live the true queen!"

After that everything was easy. By the time the rest of Abar's soldiers, at the north gate of the city, realized what was happening and came running to the palace, all their fellows were captive or dead, and the people of Meroë were breaking down Shabako's prisons. The remaining soldiers quickly surrendered.

The first prisoners to come running into the throne room were Aspelta and his surviving men. He had a new wound on his left arm, and one on his leg as well, but he beamed at Kandaki as he bowed to her. "Long live Queen Kandaki!" he cried.

"Thank you," she answered. "Where's Prahotep?"

Aspelta's face darkened. "I don't know. Nor do I much care. Queen, I wouldn't have believed it, but he betrayed us. When we were taken prisoner, he wailed for mercy. He told our enemies that he was only an Egyptian, and this was no war of his, and he'd tell them where you were waiting. They took him apart from the rest of us, so we couldn't stop him. I thank all the gods that somehow you escaped!"

"You shouldn't have believed it!" Baki replied, glaring. "You ought to know better by now. He tricked them into sending us a warning about what happened, and that must have taken more courage than staying heroically silent because when they found out that he'd tricked them, they would have made him suffer for it. I'm glad they can't have found out yet!"

"What?" asked Aspelta. When they explained, he wanted to begin searching for Prahotep himself, but he could barely walk and had to be told to sit down and wait while the other soldiers, and the eager crowds, broke down doors and freed hostages all over the city.

And they did find Prahotep in the end. Last of all the prisoners, he stumbled into the throne room, looking small and bedraggled. His face was bruised, with one eye swollen shut, and he had bruises on his shoulders, but he, too, beamed at Kandaki. He was starting to kneel when she jumped off the throne and hugged him. Then Hathor pushed her aside and began licking the swollen eye.

"You smell of dogs," said the dragon.

"Yes," he replied, smiling. "They said I was a cowardly Egyptian dog, so they beat me and shut me in the kennels. The hounds were very friendly, though. Thank you for coming so fast. I was too frightened to think what they'd do if you weren't here when they realized I'd tricked them."

"We got your message," Kandaki said. "Thank the gods you're alive!"

"How did you get in?" he asked.

"A secret passage, just as at Napata. I saw it in the Hand of Userr. I should have used it earlier, but I suppose I was afraid I couldn't."

"You'd better have the passage blocked up," he told her seriously. "Shabako is on his way from Meroë with half his army, and he could arrive here at any minute."

9

The Earth Dragon

PRAHOTEP HAD LEARNED OF SHABAKO'S MARCH FROM HIS CAPTORS, AND IF THERE'D been any doubt about whether they were telling the truth, Abar soon removed it. When she first awoke from her faint, she was so terrified that she simply cowered with her captive guards in a corner of the throne room, but when Kandaki called her over, and she realized she wasn't going to be killed and fed to Hathor on the spot, she plucked up her courage.

"My husband will punish you for this!" she declared. "He sent me a message last night, saying that you were coming and that he would be here as soon as he could. He's marching down the Nile with half his army. He'll make you pay for the way you've treated me!"

Kandaki looked at her cousin with disgust. "Abar," she said, "you were the daughter of my father's sister. Father always treated you royally and generously. How can you possibly convince yourself that Shabako was right to murder him and steal his throne?"

"Your father was going to betray us to Egypt," replied Abar. "And he would have made *you* his heiress, and you would have made some Egyptian princeling king of Nubia. But Shabako had every right to be king. He's the bravest, the strongest, the cleverest, and the handsomest man in Nubia. Apedemek gave him the Hand of Userr, which had been lost for centuries."

"Shabako bought the Hand he has from an Egyptian sorceror," said Kandaki. "This is the true Hand of Userr." She lifted her hand, showing Abar the golden wrist guard. "My friend Prahotep found it in the marshes of Derr, after we killed the water dragon that Userr himself failed to destroy."

"Prahotep?" sneered Abar, looking over at him; he was sitting on the edge of the dais beside the throne. "So you have your Egyptian prince already? I don't think much of the little weed!"

"I'm not a . . ." began Prahotep anxiously.

"Abar," snapped Kandaki, "Prahotep has enough cleverness for fifty Shabakos and more decency than a hundred of them! I'm not wasting any more time talking to a fat-faced fool like you. If your precious husband is on his way to Meroë, we have work to do. Guards! Take her out and lock her . . . in the kennels!"

"Best place for *her*," murmured Aspelta as the soldiers pulled Abar out, kicking and squealing indignantly.

"Mmm," agreed Kandaki. "But we don't have time to worry about her." She wanted to cry and held on to the throne hard to stop herself. They had come so far and succeeded against such odds; it seemed monstrously unfair that they should face this now.

"Any suggestions," she said in an unsteady voice, "as to how we, with a hundred men, can hold Meroë against Shabako and half his army? Half his army! That must be—"

"At least two thousand men," Aspelta supplied grimly. "And we have fewer than a hundred. We lost a total of fifteen men taking the city and another to the sand dragon. We have eighty-four men—and sixteen of them are wounded, like me, and won't be much use. Though I suppose some of the former hostages could help us."

Kandaki shook her head. "The first thing we have to do is send Shabako's former hostages out of the city at once. They can go to their homes and collect their own followers to help us. That way, if we can hold Meroë for even a day or two, Shabako will find himself facing attacks from the rear."

"But he'll just try to take Meroë by storm, and we don't have the strength to hold him off!"

It was Prahotep who answered. "Yes, we do," he said quietly. "The people of Meroë are on our side. *I* can see that, and I can barely understand what they're saying!"

Kandaki looked at him. She felt a little of her freezing grief and anger melt away. "That's true," she said wonderingly. "When he first took Meroë, Shabako had many of my father's men killed, and the rest hate him for it."

"But the men who were killed were all the skilled warriors," protested Aspelta. "The rest are only old people, women, and children—except for Shabako's own followers."

"But we don't need skilled warriors to hold the walls," Kandaki said, starting to smile. "How many would we need to defend the city?"

"The usual rule is a tenth the enemy's number," Aspelta replied, "but—"

"We can do it!" Kandaki exclaimed. "The old men, and many of the boys, do know how to shoot, and Shabako's garrison here had a good supply of bows. We'll call for volunteers and give them weapons. That ought at least to double our numbers. And we'll ask the women and children to start making arrows. They can fetch rocks, too, and pile them up on the walls. Even an old woman can do a lot of damage with a rock thrown from a wall as tall as Meroë's. If the people of this city are determined, Shabako won't get in."

They seemed determined enough when Kandaki went to the marketplace and made a speech asking for their help. A horde of men and boys ran to collect their weapons, and the women and children excitedly began collecting stones and making arrows. Shabako's hostages left quickly, by boat or by chariot, vowing to return as soon as they could and with all their men. And they were scarcely out of the city when watchers on the walls reported an army marching down from the north. By that evening Shabako's forces were encamped outside the gate.

The enemy did not attack that night, and in the morning Shabako sent some of his priests to the gate to request a parley.

Kandaki was happy to talk. The men who'd been

prisoners in Meroë needed time to collect the troops. Followed by all her friends, she went to the north gate, and leaned over the battlements.

Shabako drove up in a gilded chariot drawn by two white horses, with an escort of twenty men dressed in white and gold. He was wearing a lion skin cloak and an elaborate gilded helmet in the shape of a lion's head, and he looked even taller, stronger, and more magnificent than Kandaki had remembered. He stepped down from his chariot, pushed the helmet back from his handsome face, and looked up into Kandaki's eyes. "So, Princess," he said, "we meet again after all."

"It's 'Queen' now," said Kandaki. "And yes, despite all your efforts, we do."

"Queen, then," said Shabako smoothly. "I freely admit that you're a most royal and courageous lady and far harder to crush than I expected. But you should consider your position. You're besieged in Meroë with fewer than a hundred men; your friend Mandulis is himself besieged in Napata and can't help you. You won't be able to withstand our attack. You will be killed, Kandaki, and all your friends with you. But you could save them if you wished."

"How?"

"I put a proposal to you last time we spoke, Kandaki. Even though I could crush you, I'll be generous and repeat it now."

Kandaki was quiet a minute, trying to think how best to phrase her answer. "You proposed marriage to me last time," she said at last, "and I said I'd rather marry a crocodile. I was wrong. I'd rather marry a *slug*, Shabako; a slimy worm has more morals than you! Do you think I'd trust you to spare my friends if you ever got your hands on them? You have a wife. What were you going to do with Abar this time, murder her? No, I know why you're making this offer: You know that time is on my side, and you're afraid."

The handsome face tightened in anger. "I am afraid of nothing! I don't rely on foreign monsters and servants of the pharaoh of Egypt for my safety! Apedemek, the lion god, has chosen me as king of Nubia; see, I have the Hand of Userr!" He lifted his arm, and a golden wrist guard gleamed on it.

"No, you don't," Kandaki shouted triumphantly. "*You* have a magic charm forged by an Egyptian magician called Nefersenet! *I* have the Hand of Userr!" She raised her own arm, and the gold flashed in the sunlight.

Shabako's jaw dropped. He stared at her wordlessly. Behind him his followers muttered.

Then Shabako closed his mouth. "Lies!" he snapped. "Of course, she's lying. Lies and insults are all we could expect. I should have known better than to parley with a leopardess. Well then, Princess Kandaki, you can expect to die before this day is out!"

"You have to get into the city first," Kandaki replied proudly, "and we aren't planning to open the gate."

"I don't need you to!" shouted Shabako. "I will open it myself!"

He climbed back into his chariot, shook the reins,

and drove back to his own lines. No sooner had he reached them than, with a roar, the enemy attacked.

Shabako had clearly expected that he could storm the city easily, overwhelming the walls by sheer force of numbers. He flung everything he had at the north wall. Despite the arms that had been distributed to the citizens of Meroë, the walls were thinly manned, but the defenders fought like twice their number. The attackers were met with a rain of arrows. When they got nearer, they fell under a hail of rocks. Kandaki, shooting as fast as she could, still had time to notice an old granny stumbling to the battlements with a head-sized lump of rock and hurling it with all the force of her skinny arms, while her little granddaughter flung gravel by the handful. Those of the enemy who actually managed to get up their ladders onto the wall were so few that the handful of soldiers from Napata swept them off easily. The enemy fell back, leaving a pile of dead, and the defenders cheered and collected arrows for the next attack.

Shabako galloped up to the gates again, waving a flag of truce. Kandaki signaled her men to let him come near, then leaned over the battlements once more. "Come to open the gate?" she asked him.

He glared. "I'm giving you one last chance, Princess. Surrender now, and I will spare your life, and the lives of your friends; you may join your pharaoh in Egypt! But resist, and I have a weapon against the walls, and I will use it, though it kills everyone in Meroë."

"You will not get in!" Kandaki shouted back.

"Whatever weapon you have, you won't get in. Surrender now, Shabako, and I may let *you* go join your friends in Egypt, you miserable, lying traitor!"

"You'll see, Princess!" Shabako said between clenched teeth. "You'll regret every word you've said this morning, before the sun has set!" Again he turned his chariot and retreated.

Out from the back of the enemy lines rolled an enormous wagon drawn by two dozen oxen. It was plated all over with bronze, and its huge wooden wheels were nearly as tall as a man. It plodded slowly through Shabako's troops, and the enemy cheered it but kept well clear of it.

"What's he got there, I wonder?" muttered Baki, plucking his bowstring. "His 'weapon against walls,' I suppose. Do you think it's a kind of battering ram?"

"I don't think so," Kandaki said slowly. "His people are afraid of it. He's afraid of it himself, or he would have used it sooner."

"It looks very heavy, whatever it is," said Prahotep thoughtfully. "If we could set those wheels on fire, they'd never shift it."

Kandaki grinned at him. She picked up her own bow and selected an arrow. "Hathor," she said, "can you set fire to this as I shoot it?"

The dragon gave a pleased hiss. "Certainly."

Kandaki set the arrow to the string and drew the bow, with the Hand of Userr guarding her wrist. She sighted along the shaft, studying the wagon's massive wheels. "Now!" she said.

The arrow burst into flame, and Kandaki released the string. Burning, the arrow flew straight, and struck deep into one of the wheels. The resinous cedarwood began to burn at once. The men attending the wagon beat it with their cloaks and threw dust at it but could not put it out; the oxen jerked in a dozen different directions at once, lowing anxiously. The cart sagged on one side, crumpled over, and thudded to the ground. The axles and the other wheels began to smolder, the yoke parted, and the oxen ran off. It was still some distance from the walls.

"So much for the superweapon," said Baki.

But Shabako apparently hadn't given up on it. He galloped up to the stranded wagon in his chariot. Arrows flew at him from the walls, but he was out of range for any ordinary bow. Kandaki looked frantically for another arrow but couldn't find one; she'd used all of hers in the first attack. Shabako unlatched the huge bronze door on the front of the wagon, then drove away as fast as he could, disappearing into his own lines just as Kandaki at last found an arrow to use on him. The enemy fell back.

Slowly the bronze door swung open to reveal inside a massive heap of rocks.

"What does he expect a pile of stones to do?" asked Baki in bewilderment.

Then they all gasped. The rocks had stirred. They shifted again, then rose and slid out of the burning wagon onto the earth. The front twisted; the sides heaved.

"It's alive!" murmured Baki in horror.

"It's the earth dragon," breathed Aspelta. "The earth dragon of the eastern mountains that killed the great wizard Thehmanu. You must have heard the story! What kind of magic did he use to capture that?"

"An earth *dragon*?" said Hathor, staring at the thing. "If you think that monstrosity looks like me, you humans are remarkably stupid."

The strange thing was, it *did* look like a dragon—like a misshapen statue that a sculptor had practiced dragon shapes on and then thrown away. Three lopsided deformed heads poked from a twisted front; five legs kicked feebly on one side, six on the other; the stubby club of a wing projected brokenly from each shoulder. It looked more pitiful than dangerous.

Then it began to move. It limped and shambled over the space between it and the walls. The deformed heads sniffed at the mud brick, and it looked up at the defenders with blind white eyes. Then it bared three sets of teeth, yellowed, sharp as chisels, and tore into the wall. The bricks crumbled like dust.

"It will get in," gasped Kandaki. She put the arrow she'd found to her bow and shot. It sped true, striking the middle of the three heads squarely in the horrible white eye. But the point snapped, and the earth dragon went on digging as though it hadn't even noticed.

Baki began shooting at it as well, and others after him. The earth dragon almost disappeared, covered with arrows until it looked like a burr. And it paid no attention and kept digging.

"If it gets in," said Kandaki, "it will—Shabako *knows*

it will kill everyone it finds: men, women, and children as well. All of us."

Hathor gave a long hiss. "It isn't what you think it is," she said. "I can smell it. Don't be afraid, Kandaki. I can stop it." She spread her golden wings and leaped from the wall. She turned easily on the wind, shining in the light, and drifted up, then down toward the earth monster. The enemy saw her and wailed.

And Shabako saw her, too. He urged his chariot forward, and his hand glinted with gold as he drew his bow.

In mid-glide Hathor's wings suddenly folded. She fell, fluttering like a dying butterfly, down behind the earth dragon.

Prahotep screamed. He turned away from the battlement and ran down the steps from the gate tower and along the inside of the wall, to the place where the earth dragon was burrowing.

"No!" shouted Baki, and "No!" Kandaki shouted, running after him. But they were too slow. The bricks of the wall bulged outward, and the earth dragon shoved its way through in a cloud of dust. The three great heads swayed above Prahotep, then moved downward, baring the chisellike teeth.

He darted under the heads and dived under the huge body, disappearing into the hole it had made in the wall. Baki gave a yell and struck at the nearest head with his sword. The blade thudded against the monster without cutting it. He shoved it into the huge mouth, and the teeth closed. The sword broke into a dozen shards and dribbled onto the ground.

Kandaki had grabbed some more arrows, and she

stood back and drew her bow. She fired at the thing's eyes, at its mouth, at its feet. Nothing seemed to hurt it. A glancing blow from one of the twisted legs knocked Baki to the ground, and the thing leaned toward him, opening its mouth. Baki screamed and rolled away, just in time; the chisel teeth crunched the earth where he had been. The monster shambled forward. Kandaki leaped at it, beating the vast side with her bare hands; it felt like a block of solid leather and didn't even seem to feel her.

Then something struck it from behind, and it stopped. It turned. Prahotep was standing in the hole in the wall. His arms were covered with blood, and the look on his face was terrifying, though his only weapon was a handful of stones. He threw another stone, directly onto the middle head, then walked slowly toward the earth dragon. The deformed head stretched out and took him in its jaws.

Then, abruptly, it dropped him. It backed into the wall, shaking its heads. It thrust its faces into the ground, shuddering. There was a strange noise, like something heavy being dragged over gravel. The earth dragon began to claw at its faces with its forelegs. It burrowed into the earth. And then, horribly, its back split open. The great body jerked violently, and the legs all kicked at once, and then something small and pale moved in the torn back, and the huge, hideous shape was still.

The small thing moved again. It lifted itself from the horrible carcass, and the carcass crumbled into a heap of rocks. The thing looked around. Then it sat down on the rocks and began to wash itself with one paw, and when it did so, Kandaki realized that it was a little yellow cat.

Prahotep picked himself up off the ground. He staggered back through the hole in the wall, and the others followed him.

Hathor was lying on the ground at the foot of the wall outside. Shabako's arrow stuck from her side, just behind her right foreleg. Prahotep ran over to her.

The dragon's head lifted, slowly and painfully. "Did it work?" she whispered.

"Yes," he said, stroking her neck. "Now, lie still and let me get the arrow out."

He took hold of the arrow with both hands and pulled evenly; it slid out, followed by a gush of blood. Prahotep glanced around and saw Baki and Kandaki standing watching. "Give me a cloak!" he said angrily. Kandaki unpinned the lion skin, and he wadded it up and pressed it against the dragon's wound, then began tearing his own cloak into strips and binding it.

"What—what happened to the earth dragon?" asked Baki.

"Hathor said it wasn't a natural creature," Prahotep answered, without looking up. "She said she could smell the magic on it. And human magic always fails when it touches a dragon, so that enchanted things become what they naturally are."

"But it didn't touch her!" said Kandaki.

"It touched her blood," Prahotep answered. "There was plenty of that on me."

"That horrible brute was really a *cat*?" exclaimed

Baki. "I didn't believe even Nefersenet was *that* powerful."

"It couldn't have been him," said Hathor in an exhausted whisper. "It was a much older enchantment. Some great sorceror, long ago, couldn't find a real dragon and tried to make one. Poor cat."

"Don't talk," Prahotep told her gently. "Just rest, and try to recover your strength."

There was a rumble of wheels and a thudding of hooves, and Shabako's chariot suddenly drew up before them.

Kandaki looked around, and realized that they were alone and that the defenders on the walls above them had fled from the earth dragon. She grabbed her bow; Baki reached for his sword. Then she realized that she was out of arrows, and Baki remembered that his sword was broken. Shabako stepped down from his chariot, leveling his spear.

Prahotep got to his feet and looked at Shabako for a moment. "They're watching," he said evenly. "They'll all see you using a spear to kill unarmed enemies. Only a coward does that."

Shabako let out his breath in a hiss and stood still.

"He is a coward," Kandaki said. "Only a coward would have murdered my parents as they slept. What does he care about that now?"

"You don't understand. He's told everyone that your father was a traitor to his country and that Apedemek chose him as king instead because he was the strongest, wisest, and bravest man in Nubia. Many people believed him and supported him. But now they're beginning to doubt him. If he's really so strong and wise, why has he failed and failed again to kill you? If you're lying, and the Hand you have is false, how did you take Meroë with only a hundred men and hold it against him with nearly two thousand? Why have his followers died in the hundreds this morning, for nothing, while you've destroyed the monster Shabako himself was afraid of? And he made a mistake this morning, a bad one, when he showed his whole army that he was willing to betray anyone, even his own wife, the moment it became convenient for him to do so. If he now proves himself a coward as well, his own officers will turn on him and kill him."

Shabako looked at Prahotep with narrowed eyes. "Who are you?" he demanded. "The chief adviser of Pharaoh? Is Kandaki rewarding you for your cunning with her hand in marriage? Do you think *you'll* be the next king of Nubia?" He reached into his chariot, pulled a sheathed sword out of it, and tossed it at Prahotep's feet. "I'm no coward, and I won't kill you unarmed. Take that up, and we'll fight for the kingship!"

Prahotep looked at the sword, which lay in the dust before him, then shook his head. "I'm a fisherman and a thief, not a nobleman, far less an adviser of Pharaoh. I don't know how to fight, and Kandaki isn't going to marry me. Why should I fight you for the kingship? If you want to show your army how worthy you are to be a king, there's another way. Human magic fails when it touches a dragon. Give me your Hand of Userr, and let Kandaki give me hers, and we'll see which is the real one!"

Shabako shook his head. "You must be a magician

as well as a clever liar. Only a lunatic would trust your test. No! Pick up the sword, or I'll spit you like the cowardly dog you are."

Baki reached over and picked up the sword. "Kandaki isn't going to marry me, either," he said. "But I do know how to fight, and I don't need any excuse to fight you. Draw your weapon, traitor!"

Shabako drew his sword and jumped at Baki, stabbing forward. Baki parried and struck back. The blades flashed and rang. Shabako stepped back. Baki pressed forward, and he backed again. He circled his chariot, parrying and jumping, and Baki followed him, grinning, his sword making the air sing. Shabako's back was against the yoke of the chariot; Baki pressed forward, and Shabako jumped onto it. He cut downward at Baki's head; his horses kicked and neighed. Baki fell back, then yelled and slapped the horses. They began to gallop off, the empty chariot rattling behind them, and Shabako had to jump down hurriedly to avoid falling. Baki advanced on him, his sword flickering like Hathor's tongue.

Shabako lunged once more; again Baki parried and struck. Shabako put his hand to his side, pulled it up, wet with blood. He looked at Baki with disbelief. "No one has done that to me before!" he cried.

"You Nubians are fine archers, but you can't fence," replied Baki. "Come on!"

Shabako put his sword on guard again, then whirled suddenly and swung it toward Kandaki.

Kandaki saw the blow coming just in time. She had no sword, nothing to deflect it. She flung up her left hand, and the blade rang against the Hand of Userr. Her whole arm went numb. Shabako gave a howl of rage and grabbed for the wrist guard with his own gold-encircled arm. The two Hands touched.

There was a flash of blue light, blindingly brilliant, and Kandaki felt as though her arm had been plunged in fire. Then Shabako stumbled backward, dropping his sword, holding both arms up before his face. The gold around his wrist was melting; it trickled down his elbow and dripped onto the ground. "Apedemek! No!" he screamed. He turned, stumbled, fell headlong, and lay still.

Kandaki looked at her own arm. The arm, and the wrist guard, were unscratched. Baki went over to Shabako, turned him over, and felt his chest. "He's dead!" he said in amazement.

"Apedemek must have killed him," said Kandaki in awe. "He was angry that a murdering usurper claimed the sign of his favor. He is a very great god."

"You humans don't know anything about gods," said Hathor.

Kandaki gave a cry of joy. She'd been afraid the dragon might never speak again. She went over and knelt beside Prahotep, who was bending over Hathor and checking the bandage on her wound. The dragon picked up her head.

"You can take that off now," she told him. "The bleeding's stopped, and I can do it far more good than any of your miserable human treatments. If that revolting thief is dead, we ought to do something about getting back my treasure."

10

The Fire Dragon

 A FEW MONTHS LATER KANDAKI WAS SIT-
TING IN THE PALACE GARDENS WITH MAN-
dulis of Napata, crying.

On the day of the victory over Shabako she hadn't
expected ever to cry again. With their leader dead, the
enemy had lost all desire to fight, and when Mandulis
appeared behind them with his own men, they surrendered unconditionally.

Mandu, it emerged, had sallied from Napata shortly
after Shabako left it and had succeeded in catching the
besiegers unprepared and defeating them in a fierce battle. Then he had marched upriver to help Kandaki. "I
thought you'd need my help," he told her when they
met on the battlefield at Meroë. "But it seems you managed perfectly well without it."

"I do need your help," she replied. "I have nearly
two thousand prisoners to deal with, and only a hundred soldiers to guard them."

In the end Shabako's men were treated leniently.
"Even if I didn't want to be merciful for its own sake,
which I do," Kandaki said, "I'd have to be merciful,

anyway, out of concern for the country. Fields need tending, animals need feeding, boats need to be sailed, and they all need men. Too many have been lost in this war already for us to throw away any more."

So instead of years of convict labor in the mines or enslavement, Shabako's followers were only required to hand over their weapons, together with anything they'd stolen under Shabako's command, and to compensate the families of anyone they'd injured. Then they were allowed to swear an oath of loyalty to Kandaki and go free. Most of them were so grateful that they swore their oath of loyalty with some passion and offered thanks as well. Abar, when she was released from the royal kennels, was far less gracious and flounced off to her country house without saying anything at all. When she got home, she immediately sold all her dogs.

Hathor recovered from her wound quickly and hissed with relief as every bit of her treasure was restored to her. When it all was collected, cleaned, polished, and neatly stacked in the palace treasury, Kandaki added to it a large ivory box containing gold rings off all the prisoner's spears, another box of jeweled collars, suitable for a dragon, and a mirror of solid gold.

"Nubia is the land of gold," she told Hathor, "so it's only right that you should receive gold for saving it."

Hathor was delighted. She slipped her head into one of the collars and twisted her neck back and forth in front of the mirror to admire herself from every angle. "I have a silver mirror already," she said, "but it tarnishes and darkens. This one is much better."

When the time came for Kandaki to appoint a new commander of the royal guard, nobody was surprised when she picked Baki. Aspelta, who was named second-in-command, was particularly pleased. "Now we have a guards' commander who's as loyal as he's brave," he told his friends. "He's the finest fighter in Nubia. Pity he was born an Egyptian, but he can't help that."

Baki chose a jeweled sword as his promised piece of Hathor's treasure, shoved it in his old sword's sheath, put on his new leopard skin cloak, and admired himself in Hathor's mirror almost as much as Hathor had. Then he went off with Aspelta to toast their promotions, and they celebrated all night.

No, there was nothing in any of this to make Kandaki cry, but she sat there, that warm evening in early summer, curled up on a stone bench in the garden with the little yellow cat that had once been an earth dragon on her lap, and she sobbed.

"They want to leave tomorrow!" she told Mandulis. "Prahotep and Hathor both. They say that the whole land is at peace now, everyone's content, so there's no more reason for them to stay. I've given them wagons and donkeys to carry all Hathor's treasure and guides to show them into the south, where the fire dragons are supposed to be, but I don't want them to go!"

"You could go with them," said Mandulis reasonably. "The whole land *is* at peace, and it wouldn't hurt you to travel for a month or two, looking for fire dragons."

But at this Kandaki sniffed harder. "That's the real problem. Prahotep doesn't want me to come. Every time

I suggest it, he invents some excuse why I can't. You remember when they first came to Napata, he wanted to go off with Hathor and almost never came into the city at all? It's the same way now; he can't wait to say good-bye. He's my dearest friend, the one I trust above all the others, and he can't wait to get away from me. I don't understand it at all."

"Hush!" said Mandulis, smiling. "I may not be a Pra-hotep, but I've a fair reputation for cleverness all the same. I've been speaking to Hathor behind his back, and she and I planned a little surprise for him, which is why I wanted you to come here this evening. If you'll just step behind this bush . . ."

"What?"

"We'll hide for a minute and wait," said Mandu, now grinning openly. "Come on!"

Mystified, Kandaki scooped up the little cat and joined Mandulis under a green laurel bush.

After a minute she heard Hathor and Prahotep come into the garden, talking. "No," Hathor was saying, in answer to some question of Prahotep's. "Dragons do things differently from humans. *You* pass on property from father to son; *we* pass it from mother to daughter. She-dragons are larger and stronger than he-dragons. A male dragon has no hoard at all, unless he can find a mate. But if several females fancy him, he can choose the one with the biggest hoard."

"What would you do if you met a male dragon?" asked Prahotep with interest. He sat down on the stone bench Kandaki had just left.

"Oh! We would fly—fly as high as the wind would bear us, up to where the air is thin, and the sun is so bright you can't look at it. We would dance in the air and set fire to the wind. Then I would take him down, and I would show him my hoard, and I would say, 'This is mine, but you can share it if you'll stay with me.' And then—I hope—he'd say yes. And we would hunt together, and fly together, and bathe together in the dust; and maybe we would hatch children and raise them—if I met a male dragon! If there are any left!"

The longing in her voice made Kandaki's own throat ache.

"We will look," Prahotep promised the dragon. "We will set out to look for them tomorrow. We can only hope."

"Yessss—but what about you, Prahotep? Don't you want to choose a mate? There are plenty of female humans. There's Kandaki, whom I like, you like, and who likes you."

Prahotep sighed. "I can't marry Kandaki," he said.

"Why not?"

"You said once that without your hoard, even if you met other dragons, they'd consider you a beggar and drive you away. Well, I'm a beggar. I never used to worry about it, but then I never used to have anything to do with nobility, let alone royalty. When we first came to Napata, I was ashamed to go in. I thought Kandaki would be ashamed of me in front of all her noble friends, and I thought they'd pay me for saving her and send me to eat with the servants. As it happens, she has

a lion's heart, and would never be ashamed of any friend
of hers, but still, she wouldn't marry an Egyptian thief.
Whomever she marries will be a king, Hathor. He'll have
to be a prince, or at least a nobleman, to start off with."

"People here believe you're a prince or at least a nobleman," said Hathor.

"People here don't know anything about it," Prahotep said gloomily. "I don't know how to fight, and when
I have to, I hate it and I'm scared sick. No, I can't marry
Kandaki, and I don't want to marry anyone else. I don't
know what I'll do. Go away and try not to think about
her, I guess."

"Does that mean you *want* to marry Kandaki?"

"Of course! Of course! Of course! I'd have to have a
heart made of mud not to *want* to! She's the bravest, the
most splendid, the—do you remember how, when we
first saw her, when she was chained to that column in
Derr, she was so angry with us because we wouldn't run
off and save ourselves? Not a thought for herself! And
the way she was so loyal to us in Napata even after I'd
refused to help her and tried to abandon her? And—Hathor, it makes me want to put my eyes out to think that
I won't see her again, but I know it's impossible!"

Kandaki shoved her way out from under the bush.
Prahotep leaped to his feet and stared at her. He looked
absolutely terrified.

"K-K-Kandaki," he stammered, "I didn't know you
were there!"

"You pigheaded purblind idiot!" she snarled. "That's
why you wanted to run off from Napata and get yourself

killed? That's why you've been fobbing me off and ex-
cusing yourself and planning to disappear tomorrow?"

"I'm sorry," he said. "I can't help it."

"You could, too, help it! Come here a moment." She
pulled him off the bench and marched him to the steps
that led from the palace garden into the back of the
throne room. She waved around at garden, throne, palace. "This is mine," she said, "but you can share it—if
you'll stay with me."

He looked at her, and a strange expression came over
his face. "What do you mean?" he asked.

"What does it sound like? How could you, of all people, be such a fool as to think that I or anybody else still
cares what you were in Egypt? In Nubia you're already
the Chosen of Apedemek, the finder of the Hand of Userr, the slayer of the water dragon and the earth dragon,
the man whose plans defeated Shabako!"

"But I didn't—it was Hathor—"

"It was me," said Hathor, padding up behind them.
The yellow cat pressed itself against her legs, and Mandulis leaned against her shoulder, grinning at his plan's
success. "And it was Baki, too, and Aspelta and Mandulis and the rest. A lot of it was Kandaki, as well. But
I think that it was you most of all."

"As for me," said Kandaki, "if there's anything I've
learned this year, it's that whatever you are by birth, you
have to earn for yourself as well, or it means nothing.
And by what you've earned, you're just as royal as I
am."

"You mean," said Prahotep in disbelief, "you would
marry me?"

"Of course! Of course! Of course! And what's more, the whole country expects me to—apart from you, you fool!"

"I knew the gods didn't mean me to be a fisherman," he said in a wondering voice, "but I never would have believed they meant me to be a king."

So he and Hathor did not set out the following morning. They stayed in Meroë, and a few days later Prahotep and Kandaki were married. The wedding was celebrated with huge festivities. Baki and Aspelta celebrated all night again, but this time everyone else did, too, so no one noticed.

At the end of the month, however, Prahotep and Hathor set out to look for dragons; only this time, Kandaki and Baki came along as well, together with guides and guards and servants. Mandulis was left in Meroë to govern the country until they all returned.

They followed the Nile southward for a few days until they reached the point where the two streams of the great river merged, the White Nile from the south and the Blue Nile from southeast. The fire dragons were supposed to live in the foothills of the mountains to the east of the Blue Nile, so the party turned and followed that.

In a few more days they were climbing. The air was cooler, welcome after the suffocating heat of central Nubia now that the summer had come. The land was greener; there were occasional streams and shady valleys; the desert was less stony and more scrubby.

"This is good hunting territory," Hathor reported, "much better than Egypt."

A couple of weeks after leaving Meroë, they reached the mountains, the fringe of the Ethiopian highlands, with their steep blue valleys and their deep lakes. It was here that the fire dragons were supposed to live, if they lived anywhere. The royal party questioned all the local villagers, and Hathor cruised the air, searching, but no sight or report of dragons could be discovered.

Prahotep searched harder than anyone. He thought of a hundred clever schemes that a dragon *might* have used to conceal itself, and he scrambled over hills and into valleys long after everyone else was tired. But even he could find nothing.

"Come back to Meroë with us," Kandaki told the miserable Hathor. "You know there's nothing we'd like more. You could live in the palace with us and with our children after us."

But Hathor shook her head. "No," she said sadly. "The heart of a human kingdom is no place for a dragon. It would be all right with you and Prahotep, but sooner or later something would be bound to go wrong, and I would finish up the enemy of your successors. No. If we can't find anyone, I will find a cave here in these hills and live here alone, the last of my kind."

"We'll search for a little longer," Prahotep said. "After all, you'd been hiding in Egypt for five hundred years for fear of humans without anyone finding you. Perhaps there are dragons hiding here as well."

Prahotep and Kandaki were climbing a steep hill on their own the next day when the sky clouded over and it began to rain. The water poured down, and within a minute they were drenched to the skin.

"It's the start of the rainy season!" said Kandaki, holding her sopping lion skin cloak over her head. "It will pelt down like this for hours. We'd better find some shelter!"

"Very well," said Prahotep. "Look, there's a crevice over there in that rock. I'll just leave my cloak on top of it, so that Hathor can find us easily if the others get worried about us."

They ran to the outcropping of rock, and Prahotep draped his cloak over the top, where it could be clearly seen from the air if Hathor flew over. Then they both slipped inside the shallow cleft in the rock and huddled together for warmth.

The heavy rain made the air cold, and soon they both were shivering. Kandaki pushed farther and farther away from the chill water that sprayed from the entrance, until she leaned against the back of the cleft. Then, after a while, the back of the cleft gave, so suddenly she fell over. What she'd taken to be a solid lump of the rock turned out to be just an old tree, left in the cleft by some earlier flood. Behind it was a cave.

"That's lucky," she said, turning and making her way in, with Prahotep behind her. "We'll be dry in here."

"Be careful!" said Prahotep. "There might be . . . something . . . in . . . there. . . ."

There was. Something moved in the dimness of the cave. Something big. Two yellow eyes gleamed down at them out of the darkness. Then there was a soft, rushing voice, like the wind speaking. "Humans," it said sadly, "why did you have to come in? Now I will have to kill you."

"It's a dragon!" cried Kandaki, half in terror, half in joy.

Prahotep fell to his knees, gazing up at the dragon with a radiant face. "You mustn't kill us!" he told it. "We've been searching and searching for you, and we'd almost given up hope of finding you; you can't kill us now!"

"Searching? For me?" said the dragon. "What harm have I ever done you?"

"None, and, as I love life and hate death, we don't mean any harm to you. We have a friend who—"

Just at that minute there was a rush of wings at the entranceway behind them, and then Hathor's voice called anxiously. "Prahotep? Kandaki? Are you in here?"

The other dragon gave a hiss so loud and so shrill that the humans covered their ears. After an instant the sound was joined by another hiss, from Hathor. Then the cave dragon leaped over the humans and bounded out of the cave.

Prahotep and Kandaki ran after it. Outside, the rain was slackening. Hathor stood back from the cave entrance, her wings spread, one foreleg in the air, her eyes glowing. Opposite her stood the cave dragon. It was smaller than she was, darker in color, the wings more copper-colored than gold. It fanned its wings and hissed again; Hathor hissed back. Then both dragons bounded upward and began to fly. They circled back and forth through the rain, rising higher and higher. The clouds cracked, and a ray of sun lanced down, making them, and all the world, glow with light. Twisting and turning about each other, dancing on the wind, the two dragons seemed to fly up the sunbeam and vanish into the pure light above the clouds.

Prahotep and Kandaki, wet and happy, plodded back into their camp that evening. They had scarcely finished explaining to Baki and the others what had happened when Hathor flew down again, followed by the other dragon. The stranger hung back nervously from the humans, but Hathor dropped boldly down by the main campfire.

"Show him my treasure!" she ordered.

"Him," whispered Baki happily. "Oh, good."

Obediently the humans unloaded the treasure from the packs and the wagons and spread it out in the firelight.

"This is mine!" Hathor told the other dragon proudly. "I inherited it from my mother, and her mother before her. But I will share it with you if you'll stay with me."

The other dragon looked at it in amazement, his tongue flickering. "How beautiful!" he exclaimed. "I've never seen such wealth! And Hathor, lovely Hathor, I would have stayed with *you* if you hadn't had a pebble. But what do we do about the humans? Do we set on them, you and I, and kill them all?"

Hathor let out a hiss of fury. "You set one claw on them, Harakhtay, and I will bite it off! These are my friends. They helped me bring the treasure here all the way from Egypt, through more dangers than I care to remember, and they have been searching the hills for days, looking for someone for me to share it with. That is Baki; that is Kandaki; that is my oldest and dearest friend, Prahotep. Greet them politely, and thank them, because if it weren't for them, neither I nor the treasure would be here.''

"I'm very sorry," said Harakhtay humbly. "Thank you, humans."

"Don't be angry with him," Hathor told her friends. "The only humans he's met before have tried to kill him."

"How could we be angry with him?" asked Kandaki. "He's your mate. Harakhtay, while Prahotep and I rule in Nubia, nobody will try to harm you again. We will proclaim it a crime for anyone to hurt a dragon. As long as we live, and as long as our children live after us, until our house fails, you will be safe."

Hathor gave a hiss of pleasure. Then she leaned closer to Prahotep and Kandaki and whispered, "Isn't he handsome? I think he's wonderful. He says he has a mother and older sister, too, in another cave nearby, so we'll have neighbors to talk to! Think of it!"

"I am thinking of it," Prahotep replied happily. "May you have long life, prosperity, and health, Harakhtay, you and Hathor both."

"And you, and Kandaki, and Baki," answered Hathor, looking tenderly from them to Harakhtay. "May we all prosper till our lives end."